SPLIT SCREAM

VOLUME FOUR

Featuring:

D. MATTHEW URBAN

&

HOLLY LYN WALRATH

Published by Tenebrous Press.
Visit our website at www.tenebrouspress.com.

First Printing, October 2023.

Print ISBN: 978-1-959790-12-9
eBook ISBN: 978-1-959790-11-2

Cover illustrations by Evangeline Gallagher.

Interior illustrations by Echo Echo.

Cover and interior design by Dreadful Designs.

Edited by Alex Ebenstein.

For the ones sticking with us.

INTRODUCTION

The novelette has been dismissed and disparaged. Some dictionaries don't even define them as a unique form, listing only short stories, novellas, or novels. Others write them off as being "too sentimental" or "trivial".

This is silly, of course, and, with little effort it's easy to see the novelette has a purpose and value.

What makes a novelette, then? Exact word counts vary, but these stories are longer than a short story and shorter than a novella. In this case, between ten and twenty thousand words; or, horror you can devour in about an hour or two.

Sound like another form of storytelling?

I'm not saying a novelette is a movie is a novelette. And I'm not saying written fiction *needs* to be like movies. But... But they are *kind of* like movies in terms of length and threads, right? If you're willing to accept that premise, at least for the moment, may I present to you...

SPLIT SCREAM
A Novelette Double Feature

Truly, what better way to present these stories than as a double feature? Do you *have* to read them back to back in a single Friday night after dusk? Certainly not. But could you? Absolutely.

Shall we?

First, we go back to school with D. Matthew Urban. The dark halls of ancient history academia in "Nonsense Words" are filled with myth and mystery, the undecipherable worlds of the cosmos. Careful trying to imagine what those words and worlds mean. Then, we go back in time with Holly Lyn Walrath to "Bone Light," a haunted lighthouse on a cursed rock in the 19th century New England seas. If you can see past the ghosts, you just might find a love story.

Okay. Are you ready? Grab some popcorn, turn the lights low, and don't be afraid to scream.

This is Volume Four of the SPLIT SCREAM series, the first to come from Tenebrous Press. Don't worry, same series, just different logo on the spine and back. We're thrilled to be a part of the 10p cult.

If you read any of the first three volumes, thanks for sticking with us. If not, I do hope you enjoy, and that you seek out more.

Long live the novelette!

Alex Ebenstein
Tenebrous Press
Michigan, USA
September 2023

CONTENTS

NONSENSE WORDS

D. Matthew Urban

As far as most people are concerned, only one fact about me is interesting. Years ago, in the academic catacombs beneath the grounds of a small Midwestern liberal arts college, I occupied the office across from that of Dr. Paul Duncan. You may know of Dr. Duncan as the Faculty Fiend, or the Campus Cult Caligula, or perhaps Professor Butcher (though Assistant Professor Butcher would be more accurate), but I knew him as Paul, and during the few years between his arrival at that institution of learning and his permanent remandment to another sort of institution, he and I became good friends. I knew his lovely wife, his adorable daughters. On numerous occasions, I visited their house on Somerset Street—*that* house—and dined, all unaware, in the jaws of hell.

There is one other fact about me that I ought to state at the outset. I am by training and disposition a scholar, by title Professor Emerita of Pre-Classical Studies. That is to say, I am a termite burrowing in tombs, my life is shelved among the dead, and my dead are generally deader than others' dead. Even as a little girl, I dreamed of ruins, crypts, and indecipherable alphabets. The effects of all this will be apparent.

The first thing I heard about Paul was that he'd given a stunning job talk. I'd skipped it. Indeed, I skipped that whole batch of talks. After almost three decades of tenure, I paid little mind to such formalities.

Paul's talk was the third in a series of four. The Department of Pre-Classical Studies sought a specialist in one or more of those numerous nations that the great empires of the ancient world had annihilated. We wanted an expert in the history of people who'd left almost no historical records.

About the first talk I heard nothing good. The speaker was described to me as a large thirtyish man with a Chicago accent and a PhD from a little-known university in Wales. He'd attempted to reconstruct certain ritual practices of the Celts who ruled northern Italy before the Romans came. The big Welsh Chicagoan spun wild fantasies of mystic revels, leaf-crowned villagers smearing themselves with sacrificial blood while getting blitzed on hallucinogenic berry wine. The speaker spewed forth this flood of babble with an air of growing agitation, almost panic, as if he were the star witness in a murder trial and had realized, in the course of his testimony, that he himself had committed the crime.

The second talk was no better. A dour Eastern European in her late forties spent half an hour describing the contents of an archaeological dig in southern Turkey: soot-blackened temple walls, insectoid figurines with laughing mouths, every detail embalmed in lethally impeccable scholarship. In her talk's final minutes, without warning or transition, the speaker delivered a rhapsody of incomprehensible metaphysics and shaky syntax. One of my bewildered colleagues transcribed this fragment: "What here we find, my friends, when downwards we trace these roots of humanity, when we scrape into this dust of what abides oldest under earth, let me suggest, my friends, what here we find is the rootless sub-root, the inhuman sub-human, the sub-word without sense whose saying unspeaks all sense."

After such dismal showings, any display of simultaneous competence and clarity would have been a relief. Everyone who heard the third talk, Paul's talk, assured me it was more than that—it was a revelation.

Paul began by presenting a brief inscription, half Latin and half nonsense, found carved into a fragment of paving stone unearthed near the Roman ruins of Sabratha, on the Libyan coast.

NOCTIS REX / VOCTIS NEX / ROCTIS VEX

What did it mean? The Latin half presented no difficulty.

KING OF NIGHT / ? SLAUGHTER / ? ?

As for the rest, Paul rattled off a series of conjectures based on hypothetical dialects, words the Roman colonizers might have pilfered from their Phoenician neighbors.

KING OF NIGHT / SLAUGHTER OF VOICE / BORNE BY VERMIN

KING OF NIGHT / SLAUGHTER OF MULTITUDE / THE MANY THAT GNAW

And so forth. Of course, Paul remarked, given a bit of research and a healthy imagination, such pseudo-translations could be fabricated *ad infinitum*. It was simply a matter of inventing plausible meanings for the unknown words.

At this point, the talk changed course. Paul began to speak not of words but of letters, lines and curves carved in stone. How were those characters inscribed? Who carved them, and when? According to the team that studied the fragment (Paul himself, he modestly noted, had been amongst its members), the incisions had been made with an iron spike, dull and rusty, most likely around 250

CE, not long after the Romans built the massive theater that so visibly proclaimed their rule. Based on the force of the strokes, the shape of the letters, and the angle at which the spike struck the stone, it appeared the author of the inscription was a child.

Drawing on various sources, Paul spun a glittering web of theory around this clue. He cited studies of rhyming games, nonsense games, games of secret language, and childhood multilingualism. Of the flow of words and sounds between languages, between peoples, and the spontaneous formation of new languages among children in contact zones. He discussed rites of passage and their imitation or mockery in children's games and jokes. He charmingly recalled seeing his own young daughters tossing a ball back and forth while chanting in unison, "Odd and even / You're in heaven / Even, odd / I am God." He referred to his own work in progress, a comparative study of the use of invented words in cultic initiations. All this he adduced with a virtuosic lightness, as if in building up this scholarly edifice he was, himself, at play: a child building a pillow fort, not too concerned if it should collapse and bury him, since he could easily escape the wreckage.

The talk concluded with an image and a suggestion. Picture, Paul invited his audience, a child crouching in the shadow of an amphitheater, scratching at the pavement with an iron stylus. She has paused on her way home from school. She is the child of a Phoenician mother and a Roman father. She speaks two languages, knows two sets of customs, prays to two pantheons, lives in two worlds. At school she learns to read the conqueror's books, write with the conqueror's letters, think with the conqueror's mind, but at home she learns other things, thinks other thoughts. In her games and dreams the tongues and thoughts entwine, old words take on new meanings, old gods new names. For companions in this double realm, she has other children in similar circumstances. Transient inhabitants of a secret threshold that will disappear when its denizens pass into adulthood, where they will live, speak and think as subjects of an empire whose flag may fly even over their dreams.

"NOCTIS REX. VOCTIX NEX. ROCTIS VEX," Paul said in conclusion. "I don't know what that means. I don't know if it means anything at all. But whatever those words say, I suggest, they speak to us from the world of those not yet stamped with the seal of mastery. That is a

strange world, uncertain and perplexing, a shadow world. But if we seek to study the vanished and destroyed, to imagine the history of what has been erased from records, expelled from archives—what does not live in the sunlight—we must be willing to step into the shadows. That is where lost things are most likely to be found, lost words most likely to be spoken. And I suggest that the study of nonsense, of games and jokes and all such childish practices, offers perhaps our best chance of catching a glimpse into the shadows where the conqueror's words ring hollow, where the only emperor is the king of night."

There was a fourth job talk, by all accounts a fine performance entirely eclipsed by the brilliance of its predecessor. The speaker, a doctoral graduate of a well-respected coastal university, had no striking qualities that anyone could recall.

Paul always insisted that he and I met at a faculty reception a week before the fall semester began, but I confess I have no memory of that event. Did I attend the reception only to forget it entirely? Quite possible. That summer was the bitterest season of my marriage's collapse, and I can easily imagine the scene. I run out of the house, my hands clamped over my ears to silence the idiocies slopping from Michael's repulsive mouth; I drive to campus in a haze of rage and sorrow; I wander among my colleagues as if lobotomized; I return home no less befogged, remembering nothing, steeling myself for a long night in hell.

I can equally imagine myself skipping the reception to spend the evening alone in a bar.

In any case, to the best of my own recollection, I first met Paul in the hallway between our offices, the day before classes began. He was carrying a cardboard box sealed with brown tape, the word *RELIQVIAE*—relics—written in blue marker on one side. From the top stroke of the terminal E, elongated rightward like the crosspiece of a gallows, a red spider dangled by a green thread.

Nothing from that first (second?) meeting now presents itself more vividly to me than that box, a cube perhaps eighteen inches to a side, with its arachnoid decoration. What relics did it enclose? I can't say. I saw only the box, the word, the spider.

Paul and I exchanged greetings and entered our respective offices. A few minutes later, as I sat at my desk finishing my notes for the next day's class, Paul knocked on my half-open door with a bottle of whiskey in one hand, two tumblers in the other.

"Want a drink, professor?" he said.

"God yes, assistant professor."

He laughed, sat down across from me, poured both glasses full to the brim.

"The quantity seems presumptuous," I said. Raising a tumbler, I eyed Paul across the level plane of liquor.

He grinned and raised the other glass. "As my great-grandfather used to say to my great-grandmother, I'd rather ask your forgiveness than your permission."

He was thirty-five years old at the time, I sixty-four and in no mood for flirtatious nonsense. Summoning the force of all my seniorities to wither him, I fixed his blue eyes with my black ones. But what I saw in those eyes took me aback, filled me first with doubt, then with surprise, then delight and goodwill.

Dr. Paul Duncan's eyes were shining with innocence, pure and undeniable. The eyes of a child, an angel.

Disarmed, I smiled. "To your great-grandmother." I drank. The whiskey was very good.

"And to the hellfire my great-grandfather is roasting in." He drank.

We drank and talked for a long time. When I told him I'd heard great things about his job talk, he blushed and demurred. "All showmanship, not scholarship," he said. He asked about my early work, my "path-breaking" work he graciously called it, on human sacrifice in pre-Roman Italy. Brushing that cobweb aside, I talked instead about my more recent research into the so-called Tyrsenian languages of the Mediterranean, the archaic tongues of Etruria, Rhaetia, Lemnos. Paul, as it happened, had his own interest in Lemnos, and we gabbed about that island's points of scholarly interest: the Lemnos stele with its mysterious inscription; the forge of Hephaestus said to be located there; the Lemnian labyrinth mentioned in Pliny's *Natural History*; the Lemnian women of myth who slaughtered their faithless husbands and left no man on the island alive.

"They knew how to do it back then," Paul said, drunk and laughing, haloed in innocence.

I ventured a few thoughts on those bloodthirsty women of Lemnos, conjectured a historical basis upon which a later age's bad memory might have built their legend. Festivals of inversion, rites of purgation, that kind of thing. Paul laughed. "And here I had you pegged as a serious scholar. I figured you were into facts, records, solid grounds for argument. Not speculations and daydreams like me."

It was obvious that Paul was not speaking from bitterness, not reproaching me for hypocrisy or himself for dereliction, but simply laughing—at me and himself and all things. We were both drunk, and the world was nothing but nonsense.

Even so, laughing too, I tried to justify myself, to make my views clear. "For one thing, I am a drunk old woman with tenure. I am speaking irresponsibly and off the record. For another, I keep my facts and my nonsense separate. My inscriptions and attested records stay in one world, my myths and fantasies in another. You"—I pointed at him in mock accusation—"you cite inscriptions to validate myths. You put footnotes in your fantasies. One world at a time, Paul!"

He shook his head. "That's one too many for me."

We finished our drinks. The bottle sat empty. Paul staggered a bit as he left, but I imagine he made it home without incident; he and his family lived in faculty housing that year, just a few blocks from campus. As for me, I called my husband to tell him I wouldn't be home and slept on the couch in my office. Sometime in the night I woke up, stumbled to the bathroom and back, emailed my students and teaching assistants to say the first day of class was cancelled, and went back to sleep. I was well past caring what any of them might think of me.

That fall semester, Paul taught three courses: a freshman survey of ancient history, a junior-level class on the archaeology of ritual, and a senior seminar on undeciphered scripts. Three concentric circles of hellfire, some might say, but Paul swam in the flames like a salamander, quickly becoming one of the most popular and beloved teachers in the university.

I was never a gifted teacher. My students never loved me. I confess that, by mid-semester, I envied Paul a great deal.

One day in early October, as I was walking from the library to the dismal warren of offices which Pre-Classical Studies shared with Classics and Anthropology, I saw Paul crossing the campus green in the company of two students and his younger daughter. The students, a young woman and a young man, walked to the left and right of him, while four-year-old Maddy rode on his shoulders, her chin resting on her hands atop her father's head as though she were his crown, he her throne.

The group was heading for the library I'd just left. The students seemed to be having a friendly yet serious argument. They gestured emphatically, now smiling, now smirking, now scowling. Their eyes widened and rolled. Paul's hands nestled stirrup-like on Maddy's ankles. He spoke occasionally, and when he did the students stared at him with blank intensity, but mostly he kept silent, perhaps listening, swiveling his head slightly for Maddy's amusement or simply to take in more of the day, the trees shining in sunlight, the autumn breeze sounding like an ocean in their leaves. Even the university buildings, ugly neoclassical follies interspersed with monstrous concrete barracks, seemed to glow with a certain splendor.

Paul's girl-crowned head turned in my direction. He caught my eye. When, in sign of greeting, I lifted the stack of books I carried, he grinned and winked at me. We passed on, each to our destination.

Over the next few years, Paul and I saw each other in many circumstances. Faculty meetings, receptions for visiting scholars, conferences, restaurants, bars. I was his family's frequent guest, first in faculty housing, then in the house on Somerset Street, ensconced in suburban foliage a few miles from campus. After my divorce was finalized and Michael moved back to St. Louis whence, he once shouted in fury, I'd lured him, I hosted Paul's family in my own, smaller house. Several times in those years, Paul told me I was his best friend in the department, and though I can imagine him saying the same thing in sham confidence to every professor he met, I'm tempted to believe he told me the truth. Though I never ceased to envy him, I always admired him. He was my friend. My friend the butcher, the fiend, the priest of slaughter. And when I think of him now, I think of him crossing the campus green, his daughter's angel head augmenting his stature, two students flanking him like pillars framing a sacrificial altar, his blue eye winking, the mischievous gesture of a passing demigod.

The summer after Paul's first year at the college, he and his family moved into the house on Somerset Street, a two-story affair with columned porch and flowery lawn that would later loom behind a magic circle of police tape in so many luridly-captioned photos. *MURDER HOUSE! SCENE OF OCCULT ATROCITIES!* On the day of my first visit, though, the house did not loom. Rather, it shone, its many windows seeming to gather all the afternoon's light and throw it in my face as I approached the front door.

No sooner had I rung the bell than Paul's wife Cassie drew me across the threshold with a grin and a hug. Over the course of the visits I'd paid Paul's family in their grim, cramped faculty apartment, Cassie and I had formed a genuine connection. She was an effusively friendly woman, a chemical engineer who'd retired early but still put her expertise to use writing popular science articles and occasionally testifying in class-action lawsuits. A self-taught reader of Latin and Greek, she'd translated Ovid and Macrobius for her own pleasure and could recite Sappho by heart—not from memory, you understand, by heart. I miss her.

Cassie led me through the high, light-soaked entryway and into the living room, where Maddy and her older sister Meg sat on the floor, watching a nature documentary on the flat-screen. "We're so glad to have you here," Cassie said. "It's taken a month, but we've finally got the house the way we want it. For now, at least! Who knows what this place will look like in a year." She swept her arms to suggest the house's possible transformations, limited only by imagination.

Lemurs capered on the screen. The girls screamed with delight. I heard water running, dishes clattering. Cassie beckoned me toward the kitchen. "Let's say hi to Paul, and then I'll give you the tour."

Paul was dispensing vegetables from a skillet into a serving dish. He wore a blue apron, a blue oven mitt on the hand holding the skillet, a blue chef's toque. I laughed at his outfit, and he laughed too. "Why not dress the part?"

he said, and pointed to the oven. "Wait till you see what we've got for you." He waggled his eyebrows.

Cassie rolled her eyes with a smile and led through the dining room, back to the entryway, and up to the second floor. She showed me the girls' room with its rainbow-blanketed bunk bed; the master bedroom full of light and perfectly tidy except for a single sock dangling tongue-like from a half-open drawer; the study with its pair of desks. Journals, magazines, books and papers phalanxed one desktop, while the other displayed only a closed notebook and a small stone carving of a mythical head, half-human, half-insect. All was wonderfully in order, yet there was nothing of the shame-ridden strictness you may sometimes detect in a home that's been cleaned up for company. It was as if the house had arranged itself by natural harmony, like a sunflower with its golden angles.

"How do you people keep everything so neat?" I asked as we returned downstairs.

"Rules, madam," Cassie said, aping the gruff tone of a colonel in a farce. "Rules and discipline."

We dined on the back porch in the warm, still evening, with an aromatic candle warding off mosquitoes and a sparse choir of birds chirping in the trees. The girls held the door open as Paul emerged, still in his blue regalia, bearing a steaming roast on a wooden board. He set the board in the middle of the circular table, the dish of vegetables, bowl of salad, pitcher of lemonade, and bottle of wine arranged around it compass-wise. Cassie poured lemonade for Maddy and Meg, wine for the grown-ups. We all clinked our glasses together, the girls giggling to be included in the adults' obscure ritual.

The food was delicious, subtly seasoned with herbs and spices I'd never tasted before.

After dinner, Paul, Cassie, and I sat drinking while the daylight drained away and the girls played in the yard. Fireflies blinked and swooped above the grass. Around us not birds but crickets now chirped from their hidden places.

"Every night at bedtime, Maddy asks me what the crickets are saying," Cassie said.

"What do you tell her?" I asked.

"I turn it around on her. 'What do *you* think they're saying, sweetie?'"

"And what does she say?"

"She says they're telling jokes and laughing. 'Hee! Hee! Hee!'" Cassie herself laughed and squeezed Paul's hand.

"She should have been in my seminar last fall," Paul said. "The students were all bright enough, and no one could fault their diligence, but my God—not an imagination among them!"

"Two out of three's not bad," I said, "and more than you had any right to expect, if you ask me. What was that seminar again, undeciphered scripts?"

"Precisely. If any subject calls for a flight of fancy now and then, it's that one. By the last session, I was going so crazy I decided to have some fun. I tried to pitch the kids on the notion that all scripts are undeciphered." He grinned. "No one bought it."

"And what was your argument, assistant professor?" I glanced at Cassie to see if we were boring her, but the sly twinkle in her eyes seemed to encourage my line of questioning.

"Oh, you know. Take any piece of writing, from the most obscure inscription to the most famous poem, whatever you like. How do we know what it says? Suppose we're lucky enough to have a dictionary at our disposal. How do we know that the sense of the words in our text is the same as what the dictionary so confidently proffers? What if, let us imagine, the poet was writing in code? Or making a private joke, like our friends the crickets? Or what if...*what if*"—he rapped his knuckles twice against the table—"the real sense of those words is something no writer ever wrote, no speaker ever spoke, no hearer ever heard or understood? What if those words have a meaning so vast and incalculable no so-called human language can contain it, no so-called human mind can construe it? What then? Or what if the words are simply saying something other than what we hear? What if when I say, 'Good evening, how are you?' what my words say is, 'Kill your family and burn your house down!' What then? *What then?*"

I chuckled. "I'm trying to imagine your poor students' faces."

"'Will this be on the test?'" Cassie said, raising a querulous hand.

We all laughed. Paul dispensed the rest of the wine, an equal portion to each. He carried the empty bottle into the house, leaving me and Cassie alone on the porch.

I looked into the dark yard where the girls were playing. They were chasing each other in a ring, calling incomprehensibly back and forth. After a few turns around the circle, they flopped down in the grass and lay on their backs.

"Do you worry they'll get bug bites? Ants, mosquitoes?" I asked.

"Oh, they'll be totally chewed to pieces," Cassie said. "Tomorrow they'll have red lumps all over. But they don't mind. They never complain. They'd rather play and itch."

"Do they have bug spray on, at least?"

"They refuse. They like bugs." She leaned toward me, her smile conspiratorial. "To be honest, so do I. Sometimes I lie down out there in the grass at night and just let them crawl all over me. I like the way they tickle, and I like hearing them buzz. But it's easy for me, because I never get bitten. My flesh is inviolable. Don't ask me why!" She sat back and laughed. "Too much information?"

"Never too much. Bugs steer clear of me, too. When Michael and I were first married, we used to go walking in the woods, but we'd almost always have to turn back early because Michael was getting eaten alive. No spray or cream or anything ever seemed to help. And I'd be completely untouched. He must have been simply delicious, and me…disgusting!" I grimaced. "But I wouldn't have your courage. There might be more things than bugs in that grass at night. There might be a snake! Or a snapping turtle!"

"Let them snap!" Cassie flourished her empty glass, both of us laughing.

Paul returned to the table with a new bottle, three new glasses, and a round yellow cake all balanced on a silver tray. The bottle was short and oblong, its sides cut with elaborate patterns of intersecting lines and swirls. The glasses, smaller than sherry glasses, bore similar incisions. Paul filled a glass and handed it to me. I sniffed the clear liquor, smelling nothing. "What is it?" I said.

"Trust me," said Paul.

"It's from the Ould Country," said Cassie, faking a thick brogue. She was of Irish ancestry, born Cassandra Miranda Flanagan.

We all clinked our tiny glasses and drank.

The liquor was wonderful, pear-flavored with a crisp vegetable undertone, and extremely strong. I'm no lightweight, I assure you, but right away I felt my mind begin to lift and expand. The crickets' chirping obtruded upon my awareness as it hadn't done before, and I sat listening for a long moment. It really did sound like laughter. *Hee! Hee! Hee!*

"Girls!" Paul called into the darkness. "Cake!"

Maddy and Meg rose up from the grass and ran toward us. A few feet from the table, they stopped, smiling, waiting for something. Maddy slipped her hand into her sister's.

"Now, girls," said Paul. "What comes before cake?"

"A quiz!" said Maddy, beaming.

"Very good! Now remember, we have a guest tonight, so I'd like you both to be extra smart!" He grinned. "What do you say?"

"Sure," said Meg.

"Because you're both such good girls, I'm going to let you pick the topic. What would you like me to quiz you on?"

"Where babies come from!" said Maddy.

A vague sense of impropriety nibbled at my stomach. I gave Cassie a questioning look, but she soothed me with a nod. I leaned back to watch the performance.

"Now," said Paul, clapping his hands on his knees and adopting a serious expression, "where do babies come from?"

Meg's sly, smiling face shone brightly. "From their mother's womb," she said.

"Exactly right! Do you remember when you lived in your mother's womb?"

"Yes."

"How long did you live there?"

"Nine years, nine months, nine weeks, nine days, nine hours, nine minutes and nine seconds."

"And what language did you speak there?"

A look of immense self-satisfaction spread across Meg's face. "All of them!"

Paul glanced at me sidelong and winked. He turned to Maddy. "Do you remember what it was like in your mother's womb?"

"There were a thousand thousand thousand halls," said Maddy. "The walls were all gold, and the floors were covered in jewels."

"What do you call a place with a thousand thousand thousand halls?"

"A labyrinth."

"And what is a labyrinth?"

"A prison where a king puts his children."

"And who is a king?"

"A person who says the law."

"Have you ever seen a king?"

Maddy giggled. "No, silly!"

"Why not?"

Maddy rolled her eyes. "You don't *see* kings, you *hear* them. Kings are invisible."

The liquor was working its way through me, distending my mind, hollowing it out. Beneath the crickets' laughter I heard other sounds, other insects humming and buzzing. The darkness was full of living things.

"When you lived in your mother's womb," Paul said, "did you hear a king?"

"Yes," said Meg. "I heard the king of night."

"What did the king of night say?"

"He told jokes."

"What kind of jokes?"

"Like this: 'Noctis rex. Voctis nex? Roctis vex!'"

Maddy let out a shrill howl of laughter. Leaves rustled above the yard; her laugh must have startled a lingering bird.

"How did you get out of your mother's womb?" Paul said.

"You can't *get* out," Maddy said, rolling her eyes again. "The king has to *let* you out."

"And when does the king let you out?"

"When you say his name."

"Do you remember the name of the king of night?"

"Yes."

"What is it?"

Maddy made a buzzing sound. "Zzzzzzzzzzzzz."

Meg joined in, harmonizing. "Zzzzzzzzzzzzzzzzzzz."

Their susurrating voices mixed with the night insects, the still-rustling leaves, the sound of a wind that began to blow through the yard, stirring the girls' hair and chilling me despite the summer warmth, despite the wine and the strange liquor. The wind seemed to twist and curl around me, blowing into my ears, a whispering voice without words, saying nothing at all. I shivered and coughed. I squeezed my eyes shut.

The wind fell. Silence. I opened my eyes.

Paul and Cassie were looking at me with huge smiles, their eyes bright in the darkness. The girls were sitting in their chairs, whispering to each other behind their hands.

"Sorry," I mumbled. "I must have dozed off for a second."

"Oh, don't apologize," Cassie said. "It's late for all of us."

"I think I ought to go home."

"First, though, cake!" Paul said. He handed me a plate with a thin yellow slice. I ate it quickly—delicious, honey and almonds—said goodnight, and drove off, drowsy and drunk. I made it home in one piece, collapsed fully clothed into bed (alone, thank God, my husband having moved to the guest room by then), and fell asleep at once.

My strange evening at the house on Somerset Street gnawed at my thoughts for a while, but not for too long. The notions of prenatal existence that Paul and Cassie seemed to have inculcated in their daughters were bizarre, yes, but were they really any crazier than the nonsense about storks and cabbage patches that my own parents had foisted on my brothers and me in our childhood? Mere drunkenness could account for the rest, and my mind would have been perfectly easy were it not for the dreams through which, for the next few weeks, a buzzing, rustling wind coiled and crept, and a voice whispered words that were not words. But the dreams stopped.

Paul's academic star kept rising. Mine, long past its zenith, held its course toward an honorable-enough horizon. My friendship with Paul's family flourished. Michael finally agreed to a divorce. He really was a miserable man, my ex-husband, utterly heartless and wretched, and his departure shed a brightness on things. After that, as I've mentioned, I had Paul's family over for dinner numerous times, and they were always delightful. Maddy and Meg got taller, quieter, the orbits of their talk less eccentric. My respect and affection for Cassie went on growing. A happy time, all things considered.

One afternoon, just before winter break, a student who'd been in one of my classes the previous year knocked timidly at my office door. She lowered her overstuffed backpack to the floor, sat where Paul had sat on the first (second?) night of our acquaintance, and told me Dr. Duncan had been trying to convince her to join a cult.

I stared in mute surprise for a long moment. Above us, the building's ancient heating system moaned and shuddered. "What kind of cult?" I said at last.

"I'm not really sure." The student ran her fingers along the sleeves of her jacket. "Maybe not a cult exactly, but something weird. He keeps sending me emails."

"I see." I tried to look reassuringly concerned. "What kind of emails?"

"Weird ones. Pictures of ruins. Lists of words he wants me to say. Stuff like that."

"How long has he been sending you these emails?"

"About a week and a half. At first, I thought maybe he was sending them to everyone in class, but I asked some other people, and they didn't know what I was talking about. We—" A door closed sharply somewhere outside my office, and the student broke off with a nervous gasp. She stared at the floor as footsteps echoed along the hall, past my door, away. When the steps had faded, the student resumed her story. "We all went to his house the weekend before last. I'm in his seminar on ancient Mesopotamia, and he invited the whole class over for dinner with his family. After dinner, he said he wanted to talk to me about the research for my final paper, and we chatted for a little while. I saw him talking to other people, too, kind of making the rounds of everyone, so I didn't think that was weird. But then last week he asked me to stay after class. He wanted to know if I was interested in, what exactly did he say…'contemporary echoes' of my topic."

"And that's when he asked you to join this cult, or whatever it is?"

"Well, it was hard to figure out what he was talking about. He asked if I wanted to turn my idea into part of a bigger project. He said he knew a couple of people who were working on related things, and we could all work together. At first I thought he meant like on a journal article, but then it sounded like he was talking about some kind of…ritual, I guess."

"If I may ask, what's your paper about?"

"It's about Babylonian religion. Sacred geography. The Babylonians had this idea of a kind of mapping between worlds, between the human world and the world of the gods. Like a temple in our world stands for a palace in the gods' world, things like that. Anyway, I told him I didn't really have time to work on his project, and he said okay. But that evening he started sending me emails."

"Would you mind telling me a bit more about what's in these emails?"

"I'll show them to you. I printed them out. One second." She leaned down to root around in her backpack. I gazed over her bent and squirming form at the closed door of my office, where I'd hung a poster commemorating a conference I'd attended long ago, one glorious summer in the Cyclades. Blue water, tan beach, high cliffs, all photographed from above as if by a vacationing angel descending to a new paradise.

Get me out of here, I thought.

Straightening, the student held out a stack of crumpled pages. "Sorry, they got a little crushed."

The sheets were darkly streaked and smelled of coffee. I spread them out on my desk. "May I take a moment to read through these?"

"Please." Her bright, anxious eyes wandered to the bookshelf behind me.

Paul's first email to the student was nothing out of the ordinary. A brief message of encouragement about her paper, with what seemed to me a very sensible list of readings on Babylonian mythology and archaeology.

The second email, titled "Hints and remnants" and sent an hour after the first, contained only photographs, gray and grainy on the stained pages. Crumbling columns. Brick walls rising soot-darkened from weedy ditches. A stone slab engraved with two monsters face to face, human heads on locust bodies, one creature snarling and the other laughing.

The third email was sent very early the next morning. *Your Babylonian world-twinnings have intrigued me*, Paul wrote. *They touch on subjects very close to my own heart—mirrorings, reflections, reversals, distortions, one thing taken for another, substitutions, one for many or vice versa, misattributions, misnamings, what the poets and rhetoricians call catachresis. Anyway, all this just to say I'm eager to help you. You're a very, very promising student. And my wife and children were delighted with you.*

I scanned the rest of the pages. Paul had emailed the student several times a day for ten days. The early messages were a mixture of research tips, encouragement verging on flattery, and Paul's own fragmentary speculations offered as spurs to the free and playful imagination whose absence he considered a lamentable obstacle to true scholarship.

Suppose, he wrote one evening, *as your Babylonians did, that a temple in this world reflects a palace in the other. And this is a two-way reflection. When the priest anoints the gilded idol, he bathes the god. When he sets food before the altar, he feeds the god. Here's what I wonder: surely, sometimes, a temple must have burned, or collapsed, or been razed by a conqueror. What happens, at such a moment, in the gods' world? Does the divine palace collapse? Does the god burn?*

And the next day, *I know you're very busy researching your paper, but allow me to encourage you not to get too bogged down in mere facts. Sometimes the best ideas arise from daydreams, word games, idle fancies. For example, the most recent breakthrough in my own research came from a chance look at a Greek dictionary. As I may have mentioned, "catachresis" is a favorite word of mine, and I was looking up its source,* katakhraomai—*to use fully, hence use excessively, to misuse, abuse, destroy. And I saw so many other wonderful words living right next door, so to speak, on the same page of the dictionary. 1 saw* katakhrio—*anoint*—katakhruso—*gild*—katakhraino—*befoul*—*and I said to myself, let them mingle! Let them play!*

As the emails continued, scholarly speculation increasingly gave way to personal invitation. *A handful of friends and I meet every so often to discuss the practical implications of our research*—*speculatively practical, you might say. What I mean is just that we have a few drinks and talk about ideas and say things you won't read in any journal or hear at any conference. At our next meeting, I'd like to bring up some of the notions you're working on. With attribution, I promise! Would you mind?*

A few days later: *As I mentioned earlier—by the way, please let me know if these notes are bothering you, I'd be very sorry and embarrassed if so—I sometimes meet up with a little coven of colleagues to talk scholarly nonsense. From time to time, one of us brings a promising student along. Sometimes that student becomes a regular member of the group, and thus the circle expands. I wonder if you'd be willing to join us sometime? I know my friends would love to meet you.*

Paul had sent the last message early that very morning. *I have what I hope doesn't seem too strange a request. This evening, at 8pm on the dot, my friends and I will engage in one of our periodic follies, involving the recitation of certain archaic nonsense. It would help the mood if we knew that, at the very same moment, the same nonsense was being recited elsewhere, in another voice. Would you mind, purely as a favor, providing that voice? The words to be said are NOCTIS REX, VOCTIS NEX, ROCTIS VEX. If you refuse, I won't be the least bit offended or upset. But if you don't refuse, you'll have my gratitude, and my friends' too. (And just so you know, before writing this email I checked with Cassie and she gave the thumbs-up, so there's my warrant and authority if needed!)*

I sat with my head bent over the soiled pages. The emails were disconcerting, wildly inappropriate, but something in me wanted to excuse Paul, to shrug it all off as a game, a joke. Perhaps I was under the spell of his friendship, his wonderful family, his innocent gaze.

I looked up. The student's face was taut and shiny in the office's unforgiving fluorescence, her fingers clutched tightly around her elbows.

"What do you want to do?" I said.

"I'm not sure. What do you think?"

I sighed. "Paul is a strange person. He takes his work very seriously, but sometimes his imagination runs away with him. Do you want him to stop emailing you?"

She nodded.

"Would you like me to talk to him?"

"If you could, that would be great. Please."

"Of course." I gathered the pages into a stack. "Do you mind if I hold onto these? Just in case." In case of what, I didn't say or know.

"Sure." She stood, put on her backpack, hesitated. "Thank you." Turning to leave, she paused with her hand on the doorknob. "And please tell Dr. Duncan thanks for offering to help with my paper. Tell him I've got it under control. I'll get in touch if I have questions."

"I'll tell him," I said.

Later that day, when I spoke to Paul about my conversation with his student, he seemed contrite, mortified. He said he wouldn't contact her again. I believed him.

The next April, one lovely afternoon, my ex-husband called. I hadn't spoken to him since the divorce, and I tried to be blandly pleasant. "How are things in St. Louis?" I said. "Is the Arch still there?"

"Ha, ha." His tone of disgusted impatience revived in an instant all the malice and loathing I'd almost forgotten I felt for him. "Would you please tell your family to stop calling me?"

"I don't know what you're talking about. Why on earth would my family call you?"

"They've been leaving messages on my phone. I don't know why they do it. But it's annoying as hell, and I want you to tell them to stop."

"Who called you? What did they say? I seriously doubt anyone in my family would want to talk to you about anything."

"Are you calling me a liar? Are you really going to call me a liar right now?"

"Michael, are you drunk?" It was a rhetorical question. Of course he was.

"Two kids have been leaving messages on my phone since last week. They say they're your nieces and they want to talk to me. They're making threats. I'll call the cops if I have to."

"I only have one niece, Michael, and she's a thirty-five-year-old accountant with a child of her own. I'm very certain she has better things to do than leave threatening messages for my ex-husband."

"All I know is these kids say they're your nieces and they're making threats! They said they'd hang me upside down, pull out my tongue and peel me! I swear I'll call the cops if they don't stop."

"Call the cops then. Call whoever you want. Just don't call me about this anymore." I hung up. That was the last time I spoke to Michael.

Just to be sure, I called my niece Tammy the next day. When I asked if she'd threatened to peel my ex-husband, she laughed and laughed. It's still a private joke of ours.

That summer, Paul and I traveled together to a weekend conference where we both delivered papers. My contribution, fairly adventurous by my standards, aired some speculations on a mysterious phrase—*SOROMŠ ASLAŠ*—found in an inscription recently discovered on Lemnos, in the ruins of the ancient city of Hephaistia. Paul, in his much better-attended session, discussed certain techniques used in ancient texts to disguise the words of magical formulae. I attended his talk, he mine, and the end of the weekend found us drinking together in the bar of the conference hotel.

I'd just taken the first sip of my third gin and tonic when a striking-looking person entered the bar from the hotel lobby. He was very tall and wide, his body from the waist up resembling a half-globe upon which the sphere of his head sat balanced. He had a bushy mustache and sideburns, wore a White Sox cap and a cheap-looking gray suit. Stitched on his jacket pocket, a red dragon twined its sinuous length around the word *CYMRU*.

The big man lingered for a moment near the threshold, scanning the room. When his gaze fell on our table, a smile full of long, wet teeth illuminated his face. "Paul!" he shouted, approaching us. His voice was nasal, the vowels high and blurry.

"Lou!" Grinning, Paul rose to give the man a back-slapping hug. Paul was not a short man, but he came up only to the other's shoulders. As they embraced, the big man's head seemed to sprout from the crown of Paul's like a monstrous gourd.

Paul introduced us. The man's name was Llewellyn Boleslawski; he was an associate professor at a small college in Florida. He went to the bar and returned with three whiskey sours precariously gripped between his large, furry hands.

"Thanks, but I'm still working on this," I said, lifting my gin and tonic.

"Keep it in reserve," Lou said, affably sliding a glass across the table.

Paul, who'd had two drinks but demurred when I went for a third, now accepted Lou's offering with a chuckle and a roll of his eyes. "If you insist, you incorrigible tempter. Now tell me why I haven't seen you all weekend. We could have caroused the whole conference away! I didn't even know you were here. Your name wasn't in the program, was it?"

"Nah, I didn't give a talk. I've just been skulking from panel to panel, checking out anything that looked like it might give me some ideas for, you know, the project. I've been a little stuck lately."

Paul turned to me. "Lou's working on anagrams and acrostics in ancient poetry. Secret messages." He circled his palms on the tabletop as if swirling and rearranging letters, drawing them into new orders.

"The two of you must have a lot to talk about," I said. "Lou, I'm sure you know all about Paul's work."

"I know it forward and backward. There's overlap for sure, but we're coming from different directions. Paul's looking for things that are meant to be hidden. Magic words, stuff like that. Me, I'm looking for things that are meant to be found."

"Hmm." I swished the last of my gin and tonic around my mouth. I expected Paul and Lou to start talking to each other about their projects, mapping the overlap and gauging the differences, as if I weren't there. To my surprise, they only sipped their drinks, waiting.

When I'd swallowed my mouthful, Paul smiled at me and said, "You know, I think your Lemnian work connects to Lou's project in a really interesting way. Would you mind giving the five-minute version of your talk? Lou, I think you'll see what I mean."

With a sigh of exaggerated weariness, I agreed. While Paul and Lou sipped and nodded, I dashed across the terrain of my research. I talked about the Lemnian language and its place among the ancient world's obliterated tongues, the newly discovered inscription and the ruined altar that bore it.

"What were those words again?" Paul asked when I'd finished.

"*SOROMŠ ASLAŠ*," I said.

"*SOROMŠ ASLAŠ*," Paul repeated.

"*SOROMŠ ASLAŠ*," Lou said. His lips moved as if he were savoring some delicious morsel.

"That's great," Paul said. "Really great. I'm so glad you've started putting this work out into the world." He turned to Lou with a chuckle. "She's been filling my ear with this Tyrsenian stuff for three years now. Who knows how long she was working on it before we met. Her unknown masterpiece."

"I'll drink to that," Lou said. He raised his glass toward me. I picked up my untouched whiskey sour, clinked his glass, and drank. He took a sip and said, "But I gotta ask…what do you think it means?"

"What what means?"

"You know. *SOROMŠ ASLAŠ.*"

"Well, the whole point is that they're unknown words in a forgotten language, and nobody knows what they mean. All I can do is guess. All anybody can do."

"Yeah, yeah. Sure. But what do you guess it means?"

I drank again. The room's edges fluttered. My hands felt heavy and clumsy, one on the glass and one in my lap. I shook my head, and sparks flared in the corners of my vision. "I'm leaving the world of scholarship now. I'm entering the world of imagination." I smiled in Paul's direction. He was already grinning. "We're not in some dismal hotel bar. We're in a shrine on the beautiful island of Lemnos. Now, what's the sacred history of this island? What brought this place to the gods' attention? I'll tell you. When King Zeus threw his disobedient boy down from heaven, it was here, on this island, that Prince Hephaestus landed, shattering his divine body. And who nursed the broken god back to health? The old poets say it was a nation of pirates, marauders, true barbarians whose language no civilized man could understand."

I paused to drink. Lou was also grinning now, the two of them nodding as if urging me further on into fantasy and nonsense.

"I see it," Paul said. "I'm there with you."

I took a breath and plunged deeper. "Healed by babbling killers, heaven's disgraced prince set up house here on Lemnos, nabbed a nymph and spawned a litter of godlets called the Cabiri. We Lemnians worship them. And who are these god-spawn, individually? If the Cabiri are our Beatles, who's our John, our George, our Ringo? Hard to say. Their names are divine secrets, cultic mysteries, and mysteries have a way of staying hidden. But we do know what they call one of the Cabiri on another island not far from here, in another language. They call her Axieros. That's close, but it's not her real name. Here on the island of Lemnos, in our Lemnian language, we call her something else. I'm imagining we call her Aslaš." In my drink-slurred mouth, the two names sounded almost identical.

"*SOROMŠ ASLAŠ*," said Lou. He drained his glass and placed it upside-down at a corner of the table.

I was about to go on painting my imaginary scene when Paul stood up, open-mouthed, staring over my head. "Hildy!" he called. Startled, I swung around to see a fiftyish woman in a black pantsuit standing on the threshold of the bar. Her gray hair was cropped short, her thin face scowling and beautiful. When she recognized Paul, her scowl melted into a smile, but when she saw Lou, her eyes shone wide and her lips peeled back, her face a mask of surprise amounting almost to terror.

"My God!" she said, rushing toward our table. "What is it? Where comes it from?" She had an accent I couldn't place, vaguely European, oddly clipped and drawling. Her eyes were wild, bewildered. Lou rose up hugely with a cry of amazement as she approached, and he and Paul and the woman chattered all at once in a babel of exclamations. I sat silent and baffled.

Once their shock had softened into delight, Paul introduced me to the new arrival. Her name was Hildegard von Hingeloom, and she was a lecturer at a nearby state university. She told us she'd snuck into the conference to see a colleague's talk and had stopped by the bar for a solitary drink on her way out. She'd forgotten Paul was speaking that weekend, and of course she had no idea Lou was there. "It is miraculous," she said.

Lou went to the bar and returned with four drinks on a tray. I gulped the last of my whiskey sour and took the offered libation. When the four of us touched our glasses together, it seemed to me that their chime echoed in a great space, the echoes subsiding into a dull buzz in my ears. I was very drunk. An attendant was moving around the dim bar, placing a small candle on each table, and the little flames danced in my vision like alien stars.

Hildy begged the three of us not to allow her unexpected arrival to change the course of our conversation. "Please, go ahead with what of which you were talking," she said. Paul and Lou sketched my Lemnian temple scene for her while I sipped my new drink—clear, sweet, stinging—and then I went on.

"So here I imagine us, on the island of Lemnos, in the temple of Aslaš. Now, what about *soromš*? What could that be? Well, one thing we know about the undeciphered language of the Lemnians is its kinship with the semi-deciphered language of the Etruscans. And in that tongue, we find the word *sren*—image. I imagine our mysterious *soromš* as none other than this Etruscan word's Lemnian cognate. Behold, then, *SOROMŠ ASLAŠ*, the image of the goddess, the heart of the mystery, to which let us now bow down and pay our homage." I raised my glass with a reckless flourish. The others more steadily raised theirs. We all drank.

"I wonder what you will think of this suggestion," said Hildy. She closed her eyes as if trying to gather her thoughts, or perhaps to force them into the shapes of English syntax. "In my researches I have dipped my toe, one may say, into the Etruscan record. And I recall to have seen in some footnote or glossary somewhere this other word, *murs*, which means to say urn, sarcophagus, one may say coffin. So, as friend Lou here knows well"—she lightly placed her hand on Lou's shoulder—"sometimes a word, in a context of great secrets, will be turned back to front. For concealment, though not so much concealment."

"A veil of mystery, but semi-see-through," Lou said.

"Just so. *Murs, srum...soroms?* Let me suggest, my friends, we have here not only the divine image of Aslaš, entrancing or terrible as such may be, but also, too, her coffin and last resting place. *In pace requiescat!*" We all took another drink.

"I like it," I said. "I see it. Another dead god to gaze on. And what if…" I took a sip. "What if the coffin's hers, but not the body inside? After all, we're talking about the secret goddess of an island haunted by pirates, killers, husband-slayers. Such an empress of murderers wouldn't turn up her nose at a human sacrifice or two, surely! And what if it's both a coffin and an urn, a furnace where the sacrifice roasts in his predecessors' ashes? The flesh-eating forge of Hephaestus' ravenous daughter!" Yet again I raised my glass. "A toast! To the burning heart of the world, the all-destroying altar of Aslaš the annihilator, my queen!"

We all laughed and drank. The dark bar was empty except for us. Even the bartender seemed to have disappeared. My mind whirled as I turned from one grinning face to another, my own laughter echoing in the cavern of my head. The buzz in my ears grew louder.

"It all could be," said Hildy. "Everything you say. Who knows what this world has seen, what really has gone on here? And yet, my friends, we are only playing a game after all, as I with my brothers and sisters used to lie on the hills of Livonia, reading words in the clouds."

"And what would you rather be doing?" Paul said, smacking his lips, his eyes full of liquor. "What in the world could compare with this game and this company?"

Swallowing the last of my drink, my mind a whirlpool, I saw my whole life spinning dreamlike past my eyes. Childhood, youth, adulthood, and age swirled like sand in a sieve and drained away, leaving nothing. I couldn't think of anything at all.

Abruptly, Paul leaped to his feet. "What!" he shouted, his face transfigured, ecstatic. His chair toppled backward and crashed to the floor as he pointed a trembling finger over my head, toward the lobby. Lou and Hildy stood up with yelps of anticipation, and I too rose, turning with an inarticulate cry to see what had so violently seized Paul's attention. But it was all finally too much for me, and as I swung through the darkness, the candles' dancing pinpoints became first streaks of fire, then a fog of light that swathed my vision as I blacked out. All I remember is a figure silhouetted against the lights of the hotel lobby, absolutely blank, and the others' howls of greeting mingling with the buzz that roared *ZZZZZZZZZZZ-ZZZZZZZZZZZZZZZZZZZZZZZZ* in my ears as this last arrival crossed the threshold to join us.

I awoke in my hotel room. A combination of hangover and migraine blazed like a furnace in my head. Staggering to the bathroom, I found the sink full of vomit, red streaks on the closed toilet lid. My hands and face were crusted with blood; I assumed I'd suffered a nosebleed while unconscious. My stomach churned and roiled, and as I bent toward the toilet, I saw that the red streaks on the lid formed spidery characters spelling a single word: *RELIQVIAE*.

The pain in my head lingered for days, gradually diminishing from a paralyzing agony to a dull, droning ache. Last to fade was a strange visual tremor that put a halo around street lights and caused letters to jitter on the page as I read. By the time I felt fully like myself again, the semester was about to start.

Classes, office hours, and department meetings resumed as usual. I paid them all as little attention as I could. Several times that fall, I had dinner with Paul and his family, each time drinking only water. The draining, unnerving aftereffects of that last fearsome binge had made me cautious, so that when Paul or Cassie tilted the inevitable wine bottle in my direction, I shook my head with a regretful smile. Ever gracious, they didn't press the issue.

That September, I received a voicemail from a woman named Cindy who claimed that she was my ex-husband's new wife and that he'd been missing for two weeks. I found it difficult to believe that Michael had wanted to marry again, given our shared experiences, or that anyone had been fool enough to take him. Returning the call, I assured Cindy I hadn't spoken to Michael in months. She asked if I'd be willing to talk to the police.

"Do the police require permission?" I asked.

"I just thought it'd be nice to ask," she said.

She seemed like a kind person. I said I'd be willing. I never spoke to her again. I gave a statement to the St. Louis police, withholding nothing. They thanked me for my trouble. I never spoke to them again, either.

The next spring, Paul was on sabbatical, and his absence from campus marked the final extinction of whatever interest I still had in my professorial duties. I don't think my classes suffered—I'd been teaching long enough to do it in my sleep—but I skipped meetings with increasing regularity, and in March I announced I'd be retiring at the end of the year. When the department chair informed me that a farewell party was in the works, I assured her I wouldn't attend. The plan was dropped.

I didn't see Paul all semester. I spoke to him occasionally on the phone, but he always seemed distracted, eager to get back to the research project he described vaguely as a study of the linguistics of sacrilege. When Cassie came over for lunch, as she did several times that spring, she told me Paul was splitting his time between the field, specifically an excavation of the ruins of Palaeopoli on Samothrace, and home, where he'd sit at his desk for hours on end, arranging and rearranging his copious notes. Maddy and Meg were doing well in school and generally thriving. Cassie herself was working on a project she'd been contemplating for years, a book on alchemy in the ancient world. "Part history of science, part history of literature, part history of religion and philosophy," she said. "Basically whatever I feel like putting in there. Write it all, let an editor sort it out." She seemed very happy.

Early that summer, on a cloudy, gusty morning, I bent to pick up the local newspaper from my porch and saw

Paul's house on the front page. A band of tape stretched across the photographed driveway, forbidding entry. I unfolded the paper and read in large letters above the photo, *BODIES DISCOVERED IN LOCAL PROFESSOR'S HOUSE.* A terrible numbness welled up in me. What bodies? Discovered when, by whom? It didn't make any sense. I refolded the paper and took it inside.

At least twenty bodies, I learned. Discovered the previous evening in the master bedroom. A neighbor had called 911, reporting screams, and the police had arrived to find the front door open. No living person was in the house. The police hadn't determined whether any of Paul's family lay among the dead. The bodies, the news story implied, were in a state that would make identification difficult. Even their number appeared not quite certain.

Needless to say, this atrocity became the town's one and only topic of discussion. Going about my solitary business, in the grocery store, the bookstore, the coffee shop, I overheard snatches of hushed and eager conversation. No one knew who was dead, or how, or where Paul and his family had gone. None of it made any sense at all.

Gradually, details began to emerge, victims identified. People who'd disappeared at various times and in various places. Among the named were the student who'd shown me Paul's emails and, of course, my ex-husband. After that revelation, my phone rang every evening for a week, but I would never answer.

In mid-July, Paul walked into the local police station and confessed to murder. In his confession, he said he'd spent the whole day of the bodies' discovery on campus, in the library, doing research. Returning home that night, he'd found the neighborhood full of police, so he'd fled. He wouldn't say where he'd gone, and he claimed he didn't know where Cassie, Maddy, and Meg were. He named no accomplices. He said he could remember putting the corpses in the bedroom, but not exactly when he'd done it, or where he'd moved them from. He described in detail how each of the victims had died and what had been done to them after death. He said the murders had been a form of religious observance and that his own confession was part of the same ritual. The "punchline," he called it.

Not long after Paul's arrest, I was reading at home in the evening when a knock brought me to the door. Preparing a curse for whatever nosy neighbor or ex-colleague had disturbed me, I flung open the door and found Cassie, her hair disheveled and her eyes bleary with exhaustion. Before I could think of anything to say, she put a finger to her lips and pointed to the driveway, where her car sat idling. I hesitated, but only for a moment. She was my friend, whom I would not abandon or betray.

We drove in silence through the darkening town. It had been months since I'd gone to the house on Somerset Street, and I hadn't remembered the way being so devious, so full of turns and doublings. *Maybe she's taking a roundabout route,* I thought, *to make sure we aren't being followed. Maybe she's driving us nowhere, turning at random.* The trees that flanked the suburban streets swayed in a summer breeze, bowing and cringing as we passed.

At last, Cassie parked at the curb in front of the house. No light shone in the windows. The police tape was gone. I followed her to the front door, which stood ajar. She pushed the door open and stepped aside. I entered the house.

In the seconds before Cassie came in after me and turned on the light, I heard the girls laughing. Cassie led me into the living room, where Maddy and Meg sat on the couch, the older sister in a red dress, the younger in a green. The house was exactly as I remembered it, with the same relaxed yet orderly atmosphere. I turned, bewildered, to where Cassie stood in the doorway that led to the dining room and kitchen. She held out her hands toward me.

"Thank you for coming," she said. "It means so much to us."

"What's going on?" I asked. "What..." I searched my mind for a sensible question, anything worth saying. There was nothing. I said simply, "What happened?"

Before, she'd seemed totally controlled, outwardly impassive. Now I saw that her eyes were full of tears. "Paul gave himself up," she said.

"I know." I couldn't think of any possible way of referring to what Paul had done, had confessed to doing. "Where did you go?"

"Girls," said Cassie. Maddy and Meg rose from the couch, giggling. "Where did we go?"

"We went to visit the crickets," said Maddy.

"And where do the crickets live?"

"They have little houses under the grass. If you know the secret knock and the password, they'll let you in and you can hide with them."

There was a pause. I turned and saw that Cassie was gone. Light from the living room spilled a short way into the unlit, empty dining room. Beyond, through another doorway, the kitchen was completely dark. I turned back to the girls, and the silence overwhelmed me. I talked nonsense to escape it.

"Are the crickets hiding?" I asked.

"Mostly they hide," said Meg. "Sometimes they come out and play with us."

"What games do they play?"

"Mostly they tell jokes. Sometimes we play peel the apple."

"I've never played peel the apple. How do you play it?"

"It's easy. You go and find something and bring it to the crickets, and they peel it. Then they say, 'Is this an apple?' and if it was, you say, 'Yes!' and that's it. But if it wasn't, you say, 'No!' and everyone laughs because it's so funny. Then you go and find something else."

A clatter rang from the kitchen. Cabinets were opening and closing.

Maddy came over to me and cupped her hand to her mouth, looking up as if she wanted to tell me a secret. I bent down, and she put her lips to my ear behind her hand.

"Our daddy is still playing with the crickets," she murmured. "That man in jail isn't him."

My mind was all confusion. I tried to smile. "Who is he, then?"

"He's a king!" she whispered, her voice quivering with excitement.

It occurred to me I might be dreaming. "I thought kings were invisible."

"That's right! Isn't it so funny?" She drew a deep breath and released a howl of laughter into my ear.

Rising up stunned, I saw Cassie in the dining room doorway, a half-full glass of wine in each hand. "Girls, please go play in your room for a few minutes," she said.

"Oh-kay," the girls said, glum-faced, but they forgot their disappointment a moment later as they raced down the hall and up the stairs. I heard their bedroom door open and close, muffled footsteps, and laughing voices.

Cassie held out a glass to me. "Please," she said. "You don't have to drink. I just don't want to be the only one holding a glass." She was smiling, but her hand trembled, making little waves in the wine. I took the glass, and we went into the dining room, where Cassie had turned on the light.

As soon as we sat down, she put her face in her hands and sobbed. I put my hand on her shoulder. We sat quietly for a while.

From behind her hands, she said, "What was Maddy saying to you?"

I cast about wildly for a plausible lie. Nothing. "She said the man in jail isn't her father."

Straightening, she wiped her face with her hands. "Did she say who it is?"

I sighed. No going back. "She said he's a king."

Cassie laughed almost as loudly as Maddy had. "Of course." She sipped from her glass. "Thank you again for coming. I'm sorry, this must be so strange for you. I needed to talk to someone, and you were the only one I could think of."

"I'm glad you thought of me." Another silence. "Now really, where have you been?"

"We were hiding. We had to hide." She pointed to the ceiling, which still rumbled with the girls' quick, circling steps. "I couldn't let them stay. Not here, with those people. Paul had been upstairs working on his notes, then he left to go to campus. I went up there to get something from the bedroom, and...and...I saw them in there. Those people. They looked like..."

She turned toward me. "You don't know what a person can look like." She looked deep into my eyes, as if desperately hoping to see there that she was wrong, that I did know, that I understood. "You don't know what can happen to a person."

"No," I said.

She sighed. "We had to go. We had to hide. I took them away."

An ear-splitting scream rang from overhead. One of the girls began to cry loudly as the other screamed. I was alarmed and frightened, truly frightened for the first time. "Do we need to leave?" I asked.

"No. It's late. All the neighbors are asleep. Not like the other time." She stood up. "Excuse me. I'll be back in a moment."

I sat in silence as she went up the stairs and into the girls' room. The screaming and crying faded to a soft murmur of voices. I began to shiver uncontrollably. My whole body felt cold, fear licking at my skin with a million freezing tongues. I picked up my untouched glass of wine, shut my eyes tight, and drank it all down. I sat there with my eyes closed, hearing nothing, feeling nothing, thinking nothing. I opened my eyes. I was alone; the house was quiet.

After a while, light footsteps sounded on the stairs. I went into the living room and saw Maddy in the hallway, barefoot and in pajamas.

"Psst!" Maddy said. She beckoned.

When I came close, she pointed upward and whispered, "Meg and our mommy are asleep." She took my hand and I followed her down the hallway, up the stairs, and through the open door to the girls' room, where Cassie and Meg lay curled up on the floor. Meg's cheeks were wet with tears, her breathing low and even.

"Was that you screaming earlier?" I whispered.

"Yes," Maddy whispered back. "I saw a cricket."

"Is it gone now?"

"Yes. It didn't mean to scare me. It only wanted to tell me that our daddy is fine, and everything will be okay. But it saw that I was scared, so it told me a joke I never heard before."

"What was the joke?"

She made a downward motion. When I leaned over, she put her mouth to my ear again. I braced myself for another shriek.

"Soromš aslaš," she whispered.

As I straightened up, Maddy began to giggle, then to shake with laughter. She clutched her sides, fell down, rolled on the floor, pounded it with her fists. I shushed and pointed at Cassie and Meg, but they slept on, peaceful as ever, as Maddy writhed and guffawed. After what seemed an eternity of laughter, she grew silent, lay still. I bent down and brushed her hair from her face. Tears of hilarity trickled from her sleeping eyelids.

I didn't know what to do. I didn't know anything. I stared at the three sleeping forms, at the empty bunk bed, the butterfly nightlight, the star-shaped stickers glowing faintly on the ceiling. Cassie began snoring quietly.

I'll let her sleep for thirty minutes, I thought. *Then I'll wake her and ask her to take me home.*

I left the bedroom and stood at the top of the stairs. The light from the living room filled the hallway below with shadows. Outside, beyond the entryway's windows, was the realm of the king of night.

Down a short passage, away from the girls' room, the double doors of the master bedroom stood shut. Dark lines marred the pale doors, thick strokes drawn crudely as if with a fist dipped in ink. *RELIQVIAE*. More relics, leftovers.

I will open those doors, I thought, *and look inside. I will see what's left.*

Perhaps such a notion wouldn't occur to others in my situation. Perhaps, if it did occur, others would refuse it, think better of it. I say of those others what my friend Cassie said of me: they don't know what can happen to a person.

I went down the passage to the double doors and opened them. I stood in the doorway of the master bedroom. I looked inside.

The room was dark, lit only by starlight falling faintly through the windows. As my eyes adjusted to the darkness,

I saw the room was empty, the bed carefully made, the dresser next to the bed tidy except for one drawer that sat half-open with a single sock hanging out. It looked, as far as I could remember, exactly as it had when I'd first seen it, when Cassie had shown me around the house where she and Paul and their children lived.

What does this mean, I thought. *What is happening.*

It was not a question but a statement, an absurd statement with no meaning. Pure nonsense, not even words anymore. Nothing left at all. What is happening. What is happening.

Though the house was silent, I began to hear a sound. Under the stillness, behind the darkness, a shrill, cadenced laughter. *The crickets*, I thought, *in their houses under the grass, are laughing at me.* And beneath that sound another, a whirring hum like a huge saw gnawing through the roots of the world.

In the starlit room, I began to imagine. The room, now empty, I imagined full. I imagined dark figures standing around the bed, faceless or masked, or only obscured by darkness, the dim light behind them, facing the dark bed, the altar, the offering. I imagined them placing things on the bed, arranging them, and when they stepped back there lay a mass of flesh, flesh of who knows how many, once many, now one, and whatever their lives had once been or meant to them, now meaning only this. The bed, the forge, the furnace, began to blaze, or was it only the mass beginning to move, to writhe as if convulsed with laughter? And it was laughter I heard, the high laughter of the crickets, and the soft laughter of a cocktail party, and the howling laughter of the wind as it rips the leaves from the trees, and the low laughter of the ocean as you lie on the sand or sit drowsing over a boring book. They all laugh and whisper in your ear, *shhh, shhh, shhh. Be quiet*, the ocean says, and the wind says, and the stars and the empty places between the stars and all the words that are not words, *be quiet, and I will tell you a joke.*

I stepped back from the doorway, gazed for a last moment into the empty, starlit master bedroom, and closed the doors. In the girls' room, Cassie, Maddy, and Meg still slept. I walked down the stairs and out of the house. I walked all the way home. I have lived in this town for many years, and I know my way.

I drove to the house on Somerset Street the next day and found it unlit, Cassie's car gone. I didn't approach the house to see if the front door was locked.

Paul—Professor Butcher, the Faculty Fiend, blah blah blah—is in prison for life, convicted by his own confession. His family's whereabouts remain a mystery to me and, as far as I know, to everyone.

Near the end of that summer, I received a letter bearing two postmarks, one from Tallinn, Estonia and one from Cardiff, Wales. The envelope contained a printed-out photograph of a stone carving, a monstrous, laughing insect. The creature bore a human figure in its claws, another in its jaws. On the back of the photograph was written, in very neat handwriting:

Knock knock
Who's there
Ha ha
Ha ha hoo
Hail Aslaš! Hail king of night! Roctis vex!
- your friends

And now, all these years later, I ask myself, what have these strange and dreadful events left me with? What relics, what leftovers?

I owe Paul a debt of gratitude for one thing at least, one blessing. Not the death of my ex-husband, for which I can't quite bring myself to thank him, but a certain zest for imagination. Whatever else he may have been, Paul was a great scholar, and his greatness lay in his imaginative daring, his gift for playful leaps that carried him beyond brute fact into the void of the possible. Sometimes I wonder if that gift wasn't more than half Cassie's; I know she read all his work, made suggestions and revisions, and that his first published article, written before they met, was boring, pedestrian, mere solid scholarship. It dealt with human sacrifice in Celtic Illyria.

Anyhow, I believe my own recent work bears witness to a spark that used to be absent, and I also believe that, for all the horror Paul brought to me as he brought to the whole world, this spark would have remained absent if I hadn't met him. I like to think my essays on the Tyrsenian languages, published since my retirement, have left ancient Lemnos a bit less shadowy, a bit more imaginable, than it had been.

And that, at last, is where I see us, where I imagine us—Paul and myself, Cassie and Maddy and Meg, Lou and Hildy too. I imagine us standing, the seven of us, in the Lemnian temple, before the forge, the image or coffin or furnace, awaiting the final celebrant, our ultimate companion, the one who loomed up blankly in that hotel bar so long ago, the king whose coming made the stars go out and the empty heavens whirl. When the king of night arrives, our conference will begin, and the doors of all houses on earth and under the grass will swing open, all crickets and children run free, all husbands be slaughtered, all bugs bite their betters, all kids kill their conquerors, all screaming and laughing, all finally knowing that it was, at last, a joke, the joke the dreaming child told the emperor, the joke the ax told the oak, the joke you told yourself before you were born, and here, now, at last, comes the punchline:

ZZZZZZZZZZZZZZZZZZZZZZZZZZZZZZZZZZZZZZZZZZZZZZZ

BONE LIGHT

Holly Lyn Walrath

Instructions to Keepers of Bone Light, New Prospect Bay, U.S.:

1. You are to keep the light burning bright and clear from sundown to sunrise.

2. The wicks are to be trimmed every four hours.

3. You are to clean the lens and lamps each day and report the quantity of oil, taking care with the oil to prevent fire.

4. You will not absent yourself from the island at any time. If you must leave, someone must take your place. The light-house must never be left wholly unattended.

5. You shall not disturb the ghosts, whom Providence brought here, and only Providence shall remove.

August 25, 1873—

John Long writing

Arrived at Bone Light. There is not much to report except the buildings are in need of repair. The Harbormaster left us with strict instructions to keep a log of our time here. Began unloading stores.

August 28, 1873—

Mary Long writing

Arrived at Bone Light with supplies in tow by tug. The light-house is built on a small island in New Prospect Bay, which used to be called Waqantew in the language of the indigenous folk who lived here in centuries past. I have conducted a thorough examination of the records of this place and learned that they sailed these islands in their small sailboats called shallops, navigating without a compass to fish, hunt, and trade their wares of furs, woven blankets, and knives. That is, until the mid-1700s, when the government declared war on their tribe, raising volunteers to hunt them down at a premium of twenty-five pounds per man, twenty pounds per woman, and ten pounds per child. The majority of those on the settlement of Waqantew were slain in their tents, asleep, while others plunged to their deaths by jumping into the icy waters surrounding the island.

Bone Light stands atop the island, the main road (if it can truly be called that) sloping down the black rocks like a wound cut by a sharp knife. The landing for the boat is a rickety dock. The light-house itself is a curiosity built of human skull and rib and femur, joined together by mortar and round black sea rocks. There is a garden and cistern made of bone and rock as well. Are they the bones of the settlers the indigenous people killed or the bones of the indigenous people massacred? Which side of history is right? John says it does not matter so long as they are dead. When he discovered the gruesome acts committed on this island, a coldness gripped my heart, and I begged him not to take us to such a cursed place. But my John is not easily frightened.

Attached to the light-house is a hall-and-parlor style home made of limestone with two rooms and a sleeping loft. Inside it is dark for there are only two small windows. The heavy timber support beams are hand-hewn chestnut.

There are two chimneys: one in the parlor and a hearth in the hall for cooking. Over the hearth, which has a little oven for breadmaking, hangs the keeper's musket. There is a griddle and Dutch oven which I am sure to burn pies in, for I am a terrible cook.

Windy and dark. I fear the place will not hold the night. It is so lonely I could spit. Thank goodness I have John's dog Shadow to keep me company while John tends the light. John was given this appointment in honor of his deeds in the war. He served in the 20th Maine Infantry Regiment, and it was after the war was won and our dear President had been slain that the government began to award such placements; however, we were called upon only after the former keeper passed away.

John speaks fondly of his time in the war, when he was just a lad of twenty. I have often heard him reminisce of his time fighting, which he calls a "splendid cause, the grandest that ever enlisted the sympathies of man." He has often told me how he thinks the cause of the abolitionist was nobler even than the Revolution. "If I could sacrifice myself for that of John Nichols, I would." He speaks of our dear friend Nichols, who was resettled in Lewiston with the assistance of the Anti-Slavery Society, one of the most forward-thinking gatherings of both women and men.

We are not enemies, all of us living on this Earth. As Lincoln said, "The mystic cords of memory, stretching from every battlefield, and patriot grave, to every living heart and hearthstone, all over this broad land." I love the man, but how John and I argue over Lincoln! It is his willingness to offer restitution to slave-owners for their sins against God that troubles me most.

"This appointment is our work of restitution, Mary," John said as we got out of the boat and struggled up the wet slats of the dock. "It is an honor to serve these new United States, and we must all do our part." I do not see how such a goal could be achieved by two poor people, forced to live on a cursed rock in the middle of the sea because my John could not find work with his injury. He speaks of it with pride, but I fear this place will be the death of us.

September 1, 1873—
John Long writing

Cut bushes for paths, cleaned guns. The light-house is made of a wood frame that forms an octagon and is sealed with stone and debris from the island. The foundation is made of stone sunk three feet below the surface of the earth and stands two feet above it. Between the joists are occupied with plaster and glazed with strong paint.

September 2, 1873—

Mary Long writing

Breezy and dry morning. John cleaned the lens of the light, which must be done frequently to remove any speck of dust, dirt, or oil with a fine cotton cloth. While he wipes the lens, John removes his wedding ring to prevent any scratching and dons a linen overcoat. The light-house has a new Fresnel lens, a curious contraption that looks as if it was plucked from the future and set down in the midst of the tower. The Fresnel is egg-shaped, with waves of glass-like flower petals all around it. At its center is a two-wick lamp, which must be trimmed regularly and takes sperm whale oil.

Meanwhile, I poked around the garden, but its walls made of bones unsettle me much. Shadow of the tower following me. Like a person standing in a sundial, passing time. Planted some fall seeds but little hope as winter is coming. Found a copper kettle in the garden, its belly shining through the dirt like a fish dead in the water. I am so lonely.

What is needed is a spell. To douse this place of the darkness I feel in every corner, under every rock, the shadow watching over us. I say a cantrip over the garden as I kneel there, my hands in the black soil. I look nothing like the witches on the silly All Hallows postcards. I have not rosy cheeks nor ample curves. I am built like Bone Light—made of dark angles. But my mother taught me a few secrets, spells for safety. I worry they will not be enough. I will write my dearest friend, Ida, and ask her advice, for she is far more of a spellwoman than I.

September 4, 1873—

John Long writing

Wiped light and cut firewood. My old injury is set against me again. When I set out to war so many years ago, I never thought I would end up here, but it is not much too bad. High tides.

September 5, 1873—

Mary Long writing

Tide high. John carried six tins of oil to light-house. We worked the dinghy together as the vessel is in dire need of mending. Nearly impossible to drag up the rocks, and I took the brunt of it, but we got it as far as to put it on struts outside the garden wall to slather the bottom of the ship with tar. Rosin and brimstone fill most holes. The keeper's house is in utter disrepair. Set about cleaning, but I confess I am not much for housework. At any rate, Shadow is happy, chasing gulls.

September 7, 1873—

John Long writing

Trimmed light. Searched reef. Found two catseyes and a cowry, seven porcupine shells. Mary is restless. Read to her from the book of prayers.

September 8, 1873—

Mary Long writing

John discovered the records of former keepers stuffed into a cabinet in the lantern room at the top of the light-house. There have been many a man and woman who played caretaker to the bones. A hundred years ago, $1,500 was appointed for the construction of Bone Light, whose tower was sixty feet across in diameter. That is, before it burned to the ground and was rebuilt some fifty years later. The original keeper received no salary, only the right to live at the light-house and fish its waters. There was a succession of men and their daughters and sons and so on who kept the light burning, a generation of keepers with light-house fever in their blood.

How curious to read the records. On one day, the family might be picnicking on the rocks, feeding the seagulls, and on the next burying a body. The former keepers' records describe an account of hundreds of ghosts of the indigenous who inhabited the island before the colonies, as well as the ghosts of many lost seamen. Strange occurrences in the light-tower, like the light going out when the oil is full, or one keeper who lost his life falling from the lantern room when a window suddenly broke.

Up all night with John trimming wicks as oil is sluggish. I have grown used to the smell of it.

September 9, 1873—

John Long writing

Started to land timber and finished in the afternoon. Cleaned spare gears. Overhauling kerosene and began painting light-house.

September 10, 1873—

John Long writing

Washing day. Getting firewood.

September 12, 1873—

John Long writing

Mail received on the tug. I fell off the dock, landed on the stones, and hurt my hand considerably. Mary to take over writing.

September 15, 1873—

Mary Long writing

John cleaned light. His hand is better, but he's never been one for writing after he took a shot in the arm so many years ago. He said I could take over the log, if I like, so I have. Well, he was writing the log and then stood up, flung the log and his writing implement into the corner of the dwelling, and stomped out of the room to cut wood. I take it he is done writing the log.

I don't mind. I like writing.

A letter from Ida asking after our appointment and how we like it. I wonder how Ida is doing without me; if she is thinking of me. She has been caring for her younger sister, Lizzie, who has consumption. It must be terribly lonely, just her and her poor sick sister in that house where their parents died. Her dear mother was a close friend of my own mother, and they used to sit up many a night with a glass of wine, reading the cards. How I long to do the same with Ida.

As girls, we would run wild about our two homes, which abutted each other. The two properties were twin houses, built long ago by an eccentric man who was obsessed with mirrors. Our two families ended up beside one another, and Ida and I have been friends since. I often thank Providence for that strange man, for without him, we never would have met.

I remember one day, Ida went missing. Her mother appeared on our doorstep with a frantic look about her. I will never forget the wildness of her hair, how she fell into the chair my mother offered and began to weep. I was about nine. My mother insisted I stay home while they went to search for Ida, for our Papas were off to the mill, and there was no one to mind the house and Lizzie.

But I could not bear to think of my friend missing. I knew something was wrong; it was unlike Ida to leave her mother or not tell her where she was going. Ida is all things prim and proper while I am hellfire and chaos.

So I took the lamp and went out into the woods. I left Lizzie locked in my room. She begged to come with me, but she was but only six. I had the family dog, Bruno, with me, but he was about as useful as a mouse might be for tracking. However, his presence did give me comfort. He was an old dog, but a good one, with big black jowls and a pleasant face. Something drew me to the woods, I know not what. I think it was Ida. I think she sensed me there in the dark, seeking her. I followed a path, but I did not know why. It was as if my feet knew the way even if I did not, meandering through the woods until I saw a man, a stranger, carrying Ida over his shoulder like a sack of flour.

The dog was not a good tracker, but he was a good guard dog. I gasped and clicked my tongue against my teeth, and old Bruno was on the man in a heartbeat, barking up a storm and dancing around the man, waiting for a chance. When he had it, he took it. Bruno clamped down on the man's arm until his jaws tightened and would not let go. The man screamed like a banshee and dropped Ida, who fell into the brush, and I scrambled forward to help her. I gathered her up in my arms, and I remember her nails were ragged and black, soaked in the man's blood from fighting him.

He had captured Ida while she was putting up the wet clothes from the wash to dry. He saw her and wanted her and thought he could take her. But he did not account for me.

While the man lay writhing from Bruno's attack, I stood over him and said my first spell. I cannot, for the good of all that is divine, recall what I said, what curse I spent on that worthless man. But he was taken away to jail, for his hollering had brought our mothers running.

Old Bruno was given a good steak dinner, and us two girls were put to sleep in my bed. We were inseparable after that day. I heard that the man later died in jail before he could be tried for his crimes. It was a rather gruesome death, they say. He began to bleed from all of his orifices, and they assumed it was the cholera.

I almost forgot, John asked me to record account of stores:

- 4 lamps
- 60 measures of candles
- 40 measures of cotton wick
- 80 gallons of whale oil
- Tin pail for carrying oil
- Various sundry items
- Innumerable indigenous ghosts and the spirits of untold seamen (this last my own fictitious addition.)

September 18, 1873—

John cleaned light. Dusting of snow, which seems strange at this time of year, but we are so far north as to brush against Nova Scotia. Drug the well but pulled only buckets of bones and salt. Our casks of water appear more precious now, sitting like fat gentlemen on the bottom floor of the light-house. Perhaps we will move them upstairs. Drank a glass of brandy to quench our thirst.

September 21, 1873—

All lights visible. Little Bone Light from the west, Breakwater Point Light from the east, many boats on the bay. My friends are surprised when I write that there are so many light-houses in one place. But Prospect Bay is treacherous. Even with so many lights, night here is a miasma. There are other families tending those as well, and occasionally, they hold gatherings so their children can meet, but we keep to ourselves. "Don't want to be in each other's pockets," as John says. After all, we have no children for theirs to meet. Clear and dry morning.

October 1, 1873—

Received mail. Letter from Ida with news of her sister Lizzie's death. I am distraught on her behalf. Begged John to let me ask Ida to come and stay, for she has no family. He agreed. Strange fog over No Man's Island in the north. Calm seas.

October 3, 1873—

Sky the color of winter. Fixed up hen house for new chicks. Eager to prepare for Ida, who is more meticulous than myself. When we were little, she used to spend hours sewing any little bit of fabric she could get her hands on, while I would drag her, traipsing, through the woods to gather mushrooms and look for fairies. It has been many years since I have seen her—four, to be precise. It pained me so when I married John and had to leave my childhood home, and then again when my mother died, and the house was sold. My Papa died when I was twelve, and without a man, my mother could not afford to keep up the house.

Ida was lucky to have her sister, but without her, I know she has no reason to stay in her home. The sale will give her enough to live on for the rest of her life, independently, with no man necessary to keep her safe. As I cut wire for the chicks, I imagined what that must feel like—complete independence to go wherever she likes. And she chose to come here, to me, on this bleak, black island in the middle of the cold, dark sea.

I was much distracted and cut my hand on the wire. Ah well, a bit of blood spent will protect the chicks, after all.

October 5, 1873—

John has always been a quiet man. He is not harsh like some men, who might raise a hand against their wives for the littlest of grievances. He has always been a man who puts his efforts into the things he does, and for this, I appreciate him. He has never asked about how I came to be who I am today, or how I met Ida, or what kinds of emotions I feel. What need has he of such things? But he is steady like the light, and he has given me a good home. Sometimes he laughs at me when I struggle with things like the housework. Not in an unkindly way, but in a way that lets me know he loves me.

It is a strange world to live in as a woman. I know all the things John does, but he seems to only allow me to help with a kind of gruff acknowledgment. Some men would not want their wives painting dinghies and repairing the walls. They would assign them only the task of that which is soft—sewing clothing or washing clothing or caring for the hens. Of course, I do these things too, but I am not as good at them as I would like to admit. John doesn't hold me accountable for anything. And yet I still know how he feels about me.

Like when I asked about Ida, there was a tone in his voice that was a bit like the tone you use when you speak to a child. "If it would grant you peace, Mary, then yes," he said. When he took me away from Ida, I don't think he realized he was taking me away from my whole world. But this is normal, for a young wife with a new husband and many cares to tend to and a home to keep. I know I should be grateful.

How strange to go about life with not a care in the world. Yesterday I had to call him in from the woodshed where he was making a sink out of tin and wood. It was dark as night comes early, but he still stood out there, banging away. When I asked him why he didn't come in earlier, he just shrugged. No concept of space and time whatsoever. Oh to be a man!

October 9, 1873—

Yesterday a ship wrecked on the rocks of No Man's Island, and John rowed out but found no survivors or bodies. It is the most curious thing. The day was bright and clear. We could not make head nor tail of why the ship did not stop despite our signaling with the flag, ringing of the bell, and flashing of the light. Replenished oil while John was gone and trimmed wicks. Lens is covered in black soot. Must ask John to wipe it more regularly or perhaps use some glycerin.

October 12, 1873—

John wiped lens. Waves timid this morning. I worked in the garden, and I saw the ghost of an indigenous woman. A light flashed, and I looked up, thinking John had lit the lamp in the day for some reason. I saw a figure standing in the sunlight, a shadow outlined. She was pregnant, her belly wide as she stood in the garden with her hands on her hips, as if she'd just put down some women's work for a respite. She began to play with a great hoop made of bent wood and woven with reeds. It spun and spun, catching the sun, whirling brighter and brighter, faster and faster.

John found me in the garden, my head drenched in blood. I must have fallen and hit my head. Sick all night. Did the woman mean me harm? Or was she trying to warn me?

October 17, 1873—

Received mail and food allowance. Letter from Ida, who is coming within the fortnight. Much reminiscing of our days as girls at school and of our mothers, who dearly loved each other and encouraged our friendship. Her letter brought tears to my eyes, with memories swimming in my mind. I must dig out my mother's spellbook from my things, but with all the work, there has not been much time to set things to rights.

Record of provisions:

- 100 lbs pork
- 50 lbs beef
- 25 lbs sugar
- 2 barrels flour
- 15 lbs coffee
- 5 lbs beans
- 2 gls vinegar – short from 4
- 1 barrel potatoes
- 10 lbs rice
- 10 oz mustard powder, salt, pepper

October 20, 1873—

John cleaned light. All lights visible. Emptied stores into storage and made up barrel for rainwater. We find very little time to get lonely now. John holds conference with the ghosts of keepers past. I watch him from the cot in the top of the tower, tucked under my mother's old quilt, which I could not bear to leave behind, as he sits in his rocking chair, head tilted to listen to their voices while he reads aloud the instructions set forth by his predecessors.

He is going gray at the temples, and it touches me to see him speak to the ghosts in a low voice.

October 25, 1873—

Small wreck of four local boys. One was swinging from the mast, and they capsized. John took the dinghy out and threw a line to them, bringing them onto the boat, but could make no headway back. He rounded the spit, but the winds were too strong. I signaled for him to drop anchor. When the tide receded, he was able to bring them on land. We keep survivors three at a time in the loft of the keeper's house, never in our stone and bone light-house. We also keep them in provisions and tales. Later, John rowed them out to the mainland, he and the boys all laughing and joking like sailors do. He came back in the afternoon, his face ruddy and cheerful. He brought me back a ladies' magazine and said, "I know how you like to look at the outfits." What a dear thing to do. Of course, I could not care less about such things, but I tucked a smile into my apron and put the magazine aside.

October 27, 1873—

Breezy morn. I know John wishes we could have children, although I've told him I am not interested, and besides the fact that we have had no luck thus far and perhaps never will. It is not for lack of trying. He is still speaking of the raucous boys from yesterday and the things they told him, as boys do, of their adventures on the coast. One of the boys gave him a little comb and oil for his hair and beard. He did himself up right and put on his one suit, and I put on my pink dress, and we danced with the music of the waves outside, delirious on brandy and his good humor. I write this now, and I admit I am a bit drunk. I cannot give John what he wants, but I love him still. It will be better when Ida comes. There will not be just the two of us bashing about at each other like apples in a barrel.

October 29, 1873—

A great crash and Shadow barking in the night. Found John sprawled at the top of the tower stairs with a bloody head. I believe a lamp fell on him, but his speech is gone. He is much burned. Wrapped his wounds and head and put him to bed in the cot—there is no likely way I could carry him down to the keeper's house. Cleaned light.

October 31, 1873—

All Hallows. My dear John has gone to God.

The ladies magazines have tips for parties on All Hallows. A recipe for a soul cake. I stoke the little stove and put one in to bake while I sit to write this. Back home, All Hallows was a night for young maidens to try out their future husbands, taking them into the night for tricks and giving each other a crooked sixpence. Mother used to fasten a horseshoe to the door made of iron, she said to ward away the fairies or evil spirits. There would be a good supper, a concert, or a ball. My mother and Ida's would play snapdragon—dousing a bowl of raisins in brandy and lighting it afire, then reaching in to try and grasp a raisin, a feat requiring much courage and quickness of hand to achieve. "Snip, snap, dragon!" She used to laugh as we chanted the old song. Father used to call her games and superstitions foolish, preferring his Christian upbringing. Did he know what lay beside him each night in bed? Did he know of mother's spellbook, kept under her pillow?

I met John at an All Hallows party. There was a fortune teller there, an older woman who put on makeup to make herself the crone. She wore a pointed dark hood and told the cards. When I stepped into her little tent, which she had put up outside the town hall to catch the revelers on their entry, she took a sharp breath in. Her old hands wrapped around mine, and she said, "Your love waits for you tonight." I thought nothing of her words, being young and hot from our brisk walk to the hall, Ida and I. There were nuts burning on the fire, and love tests, and my heart was too hard, I thought, for any man to turn it. When we went inside the hall, it was warm with bodies, and my eyes latched onto John, and indeed, my head did spin. Only now, I wonder what the fortune teller said to Ida. I never asked her that night. Perhaps I should have.

I have burned the cake in my reminiscence. John is dead upstairs by the light. Did my longing for Ida kill him? Or was it the ghosts? How will I get him down the stairs? I must, though. I cannot leave him to rot there in the cot. I sat by his side all night except on the third hours when I needed to trim the wicks. His last words to me were, "Mind the light, Mary." He went with his eyes open, staring at that cursed light. I felt his spirit carried to God, or whatever divine thing has control over this wretched world.

Cleaned light and wiped lens, replenished oil stores.

November 1, 1873—

Fresh morning. Dug a grave for my dear John. I will write to my brother and ask him to recommend me to the posting of keeper. I read that only women who are widows may be keepers, and now here I am. I hope my brother does not insist on coming. I do not think he will; he is much preoccupied with his bid for local governance. Meanwhile, I must take up John's duties. Cut firewood.

November 2, 1873—

Capricious waves. So little time to write this. Worked dinghy, which is now in better order. As soon as I had it down in the water, I caught sight of a military boat. I tied the boat and ran up to ring the bell. The rope to the bell broke, and I climbed up into the rafters to hammer the bell, but the ship did not seem to hear. I kept ringing, out of my mind. Why did they not hear the bell? She crashed on the rocks. Dead sailors on the shore. Hundreds of them. I keep them, too.

November 4, 1873—

Fantastic storm. Waves so high they threaten to wash me away. I worry about Ida traveling to join me. The thought of her cheerful face keeps me working. During windy nights, it is very near impossible to keep the light burning. It is almost as if I am standing in a tunnel of light, and then everything goes dark, and I must work to light the lamp again. I sleep on the cot in the lantern room and keep one eye on the light even as I sleep.

November 5, 1873—

Several planks on the dock washed away by the storm. I put out new ones and then went back to digging graves. I know now why there are so many bones and ghosts on this island. It draws death to it. My arms ache to write this. The sailors were so young. As I lay each body in the earth, I keep thinking, will you come back to haunt me? Who did you belong to? Whose child were you?

All lights visible.

November 6, 1873—

Bright and brisk day. Finished hen house repairs. The girls seem happy to have a warm place to rest their feathers. The dog lay down before the house to guard it. Began painting the keeper's house for Ida's coming. Went and had a yearn over John's old clothing. Perhaps I will fix them up for myself to wear. John was not much taller than myself, and pants are more practical for the work.

November 6, 1873—

Warm weather. Cleaned light, sewed curtains for the parlor out of John's old shirts, which will help keep the light out at night for Ida; also, she will laugh at my clumsy sewing. Wrote to the Harbormaster to request stores of cloth to make a keeper's coat—blue cloth and yellow trim. Several fishermen passed by.

November 7, 1873—

Woke this morning to a clear blue sky and the sound of laughter on the water. Ida came with the mailboat, standing on its prow with her dark, curly hair dancing in the wind and her smile like a star over the sea. She stepped off the boat and handed me the letter pronouncing me keeper with a salary of $750 a year. When the mailboat was gone around No Man's Island, I swept her up in my arms and hugged her something fierce. She laughed upon seeing the shabby curtains and quickly set about cleaning the parlor. Old Shadow was dancing about with joy to see her, even though he didn't know her. He kept at her side all day like his name suggests. Showed Ida the light and began teaching her how to set the lamp and how to clean the reflector.

Ida is like a breeze on a sunny day. She looked upon the graves and then said, "Oh Mary," and just the gentleness of the way she said it made me want to cry. Of course, I did not. She promised me we would have a service for John, to lay his soul to rest. But I shook my head. I do not want him gone from me. I want his spirit here, in his final place, with the light he so cared for. Ida does not push.

November 13, 1873—

Hazy morn. Taught Ida the care of the oil, my constant occupation. Ida remarked that the roof of the keeper's house is leaking, and outbuildings are wanted, including a washroom. I have been so preoccupied that when she pointed out a rather drab painting in the bedroom of a sinking wreck, I nearly ate my tongue. I'd never noticed the dull thing. Ida is a force for good, helping to cut wood for repairs and never ceasing to find a joke to make. She cheers me much.

November 15, 1873—

Showed Ida my reports. I record more than I ought. A keeper's log should be the weather and the tasks of the day, nothing more or less. What will the Harbormaster think of my talk of witchcraft? Perhaps I should tell Ida to burn the log if I die. We rarely report the saving of seamen due to all the confounded paperwork. Cleaned light.

November 16, 1873—

Ida brought a phonograph among her many feminine knickknacks. She says she knows she will miss the sound of human voices out here on the harbor, alone except for the lights. I enjoyed the opera she played this evening and was lulled into sleep, only to awake and find Shadow at my feet and Ida up in the tower, maintaining the light. Worry left me, and I let myself drift, thinking of John. I wonder if he would be pleased to see how we are getting on without him. I visited his grave and tried to plant some flowers there, but the dirt is not very good. Stone and bone and cursed soil.

November 18, 1873—

Dry and calm morn. Cleaned light. The mailboat came by but did not stop. We set about putting the garden in order. Ida digs in the dirt and pulls out bones upon bones. The history I am reading that covers this bay and nearby islands tells of the massacre of the indigenous people and the many wrecks this island has endured. How could John read such a thing and want to bring his young wife here? There are records of the indigenous rituals, "smudging" herbs and other greenery tied up in a bundle and lit afire, the smoke spread over a body to keep it at peace, or in a home to keep out bad spirits. It sounds like my mother's ritual for cleansing a house. Ida, in her neat apron with her hair tied up, takes the bones and gently sets them aside for use in shoring up the walls of the garden, which protect the plants from the constant winds. She has found the seedlings I planted haphazardly when I first arrived; I was shocked to see the little things had survived. I feel that with Ida here, perhaps something more will grow.

November 20, 1873—

On this day, we woke early in the darkness before dawn to watch the expected great comet, which was foretold in the Almanac to strike the Earth and devastate all things terrestrial. Ida has a little telescope, and we huddled together at the top of the tower on the gallery, taking turns watching the comet streak through the sky. Of course, it missed Earth and passed through the stars in a white streak. The comet was said to portend all sorts of woes, but it merely made me hungry.

November 21, 1873—

Cleaned light, arranged stores. Provisions low. I will write and ask for Ida to be appointed as my assistant, providing some extra funds for the building of additional structures. Military boats passing on the water waved to the "little ladies of the light." We waved back and then sat by the light, telling stories of our childhood.

"Do you remember the spell to keep all things safe?" Ida asked me.

I nodded, fighting with my sewing again.

Ida's sat neatly on her lap, her hands always working away with the needle while I struggled to just keep my stitches straight. "I took mother's book when I left." She pulled it out of her pocket and it to me. "It is much like your mother's, I imagine."

I leafed through her mother's book and smiled. She was like an aunt to me when she was alive. It is rather a domestic little book, and it reminds me of Ida's style of spells. Neat little bits of craft that keep the house clean and organized. My mother's is rather rougher but has less depth.

I came upon a spell for keeping all things safe. How can such a spell work, I wonder? The spell claims to cast a net of safety over a place. It is quite complex. The hardest part is that it requires an empty vessel. A human who has lost their spirit. Does it mean the person's spirit is broken, or that their soul has left their body entirely? The person draws the evil within them and fights it until it is destroyed inside the vessel's skin. Then, the evil is released, and the vessel is cleansed.

I read aloud what Ida's mother wrote, in her keen little handwriting. "The spell extends to a radius of several miles in every direction. I witnessed a successful casting when I was just a girl. A woman in our village went mad, and the coven took her into their light and cast out the demons hidden in her skin. The clergy wanted to exorcise her, but the witches got to her first. She came back to herself and was sent back to her family, whole and at peace. For a period of thirty years, the village knew no sickness nor unnatural death. No one was murdered and no accidents befell the villagers. Beyond the boundaries of the village was another matter."

"Do you think it would help this—" Ida started.

A sound outside cut off Ida's words. A crashing. We went to the light-house and saw one of the barrels of water had burst as if shot by a cannon. We saw no ghosts, but they were there, invisible. We stood shivering in the dusk and Ida took my hand for a moment.

"How could we do it?" I whispered as we picked up the pieces of the barrel. "There is no vessel. It is just us."

I met Ida's eyes, and they were fierce, but I knew she agreed. We need a vessel if we want to cleanse this place.

November 22, 1873—

I cannot tell when I love the sea the most—in a calm and quiet mood or at her most restless rage. Ida is much the same. She watches me with a quirk in her smile and then catches me off guard, dragging me to the house to play cards or listen to her music. I remember her being this way when we played together as girls, making up grand stories of our adventures when we were to grow up. Bone

Light seems to understand her, and she is a sight to behold standing against the railing of the gallery as she extends a lamp out over the sea far below, her hair wild about her face, her eyes piercing the night to search for vessels and to check the nearby lights.

November 26, 1873—

Hard seas. Bone Light is bewitched tonight. I am up every hour checking the oil, for the light is always flickering low, and the wind outside seems to whip it into a frenzy despite the glass. It is as if the light can sense something out there. I sent Ida to check for vessels. The fog signal went out, and so Ida took up the hammer, I took up the flags, and we guided three local vessels to safe harbor. The reflector must be wiped over as winter comes upon us, the smoke from the stove leaves a thin grime on its surface.

Exhausted. I keep thinking how much easier things would be if John were still alive. But I can't let myself think about those things. Lately, I have been sensing his presence. I awake in the night looking for him but find only the light. Ida asks me if I want her to sleep with me in the little cot beside the light, the place where I used to watch John. "I will watch over you while you tend the light. We could take turns." It is a tempting thought. But the light is my responsibility; John left it to me.

November 28, 1873—

Strong breeze from N.W. and light rain. Ida conjured up a fishing pole she made from her bits and bobs. We caught several large fish and made them up on the bonfire for dinner. Ida is a much better cook than myself. Several steamers passed and made it safely in. Laid up reading our two spellbooks, my mother's and Ida's mother's, most of the day.

The vessel must be strong to survive the spell, like a boat at sea that must survive a great storm. I do not know who might do it. I could write my brother to come and stay with us, but I don't know. I like being here with just Ida. I know not what to do about this place. I just know it will be the death of me if something is not done.

I scoured the old light-house keepers' records, thinking perhaps one of them, or their wives, was skilled in spellwork, but found nothing promising.

"Do you recall the day with the fortune teller?" I asked Ida.

"Of course," she replied. "It was the day you met John."

"Yes," I said. I buried my face in my apron as if I was wiping sea spray from my skin. My apron smelled like flour and apples. "What did the fortune teller tell you?"

Ida put her book down. "What a strange time to ask."

I said nothing but felt my throat tighten.

"She was a true practitioner, that old artist." Ida ran her hand over the leather-bound book. "She told me that I would meet my true love that night."

"That's what she told *me*."

"I know."

I hesitate. "So, did you?"

"I already had met my true love."

I went out into the garden before I could allow myself to reply. My head felt like it was floating, like my legs were made of clouds. Ida! Does she know what her words meant to me, how they cut me to my heart?

If I had known what the fortune teller had told Ida and what her reply had been, would things have turned out differently? We certainly never would have made it to Bone Light together.

It's not worth it, obsessing over what might have been. My John is gone, and we lived a good life together, and now I am living a good life with Ida.

I found myself stomping back into the parlor, tracking mud over the rug, but Ida merely raised her eyebrows at me. "Are you staying forever?" I asked, my voice hot. "Can I count on you to stay? Are we—" the words got all choked up in me. "Are we friends? Are we—something else?"

Ida put her head back and laughed, and the curve of her throat burned in my sight. "Oh, Mary," she said, "I am not going anywhere." And she went back to reading as if that was that.

I flew from the parlor, lighter than air. Suddenly the strange tower seemed familiar and silly, quaint even. I danced around the garden with Shadow, his barks muffled by the rain.

December 1, 1873—

Cloudy but dry with a light breeze. Cleaned light and various duties. Received letter from light-house district stating that the inspector is expected to visit us in the fortnight. Oiled mast of the dinghy and laid some lead to soak.

December 2, 1873—

Woken in the night by the sound of muffled oars. Prowlers on the shore—three men creeping their way up the rocks with a light. Even thieves would die on those rocks without a light. I went out on the gallery and emptied the contents of the chamber pot onto their heads while Ida held them at bay with John's old rifle, which I know for a fact to be without shot. In the morning, Ida will row them to Barnstable and the constable.

December 3, 1873—

The men who tried to overtake the light-house insist they were seeking treasures left behind by the indigenous peoples of this island. Ida told them they should read less papers, and I told them they were lucky to be alive. We commandeered their boat. It is a clever little craft, and with some tar I will find it useful to have a larger boat in case there is a need for two. "What nonsense," Ida called as we rowed across the calm water. "As if the indigenous people weren't driven out of this land by folks like those men." I think she is probably right.

December 5, 1873—

Ida does not feel unsettled by the ghosts of Bone Light. She walks among the garden and speaks to them, laying her hand gently on their bones or whistling a tune that makes Shadow whine. It is a pleasure to watch her with her keen eyes searching in the dirt for a bit of bone to fit the perfect spot in the wall. Her spells are stronger than mine, and where she lays her hands, there seems to be a kind of gentle mist, a pooling of warmth. I treasure her footprints in the snow. The light seems less restless with her here. I am less restless too.

"It is not just the ghosts of the indigenous people here," Ida said. "It is the ghosts of every soul that has passed through this area. But I do not believe it was a cursed place always. I believe once, green things grew here. Who knows why such places become evil?"

"Man. Men. Women sometimes, too," I said.

Ida stepped close to me, and my heart pounded, flopping in my chest like a fish. "Mary," she whispered.

I will take this out later. I will burn this page so no one can see it but me. No one need feel the touch of Ida's lips brushing mine. No one need know how she untied the laces of my dress with dexterous fingers. No one need know the light burning between us.

December 8, 1873—

Visit from light-house inspector who came on the mailboat. He is a fastidious little man with a thin and greasy mustache. He complained loudly of the dirty oil (no mind that it is all we have received from the district), the general disrepair of the keeper's house, the chipped coating on the lens, and the shoddy construction of the lamps. He seemed ill at ease among us women and said he would request a man be appointed to Bone Light posthaste.

After tea, we put him to bed in the loft, and we slept on the cot up by the light, neither being quite proper, but neither of us wanting to be in the same room with that hawkshaw sniffing about, touching our things.

Lying beside me in the brightness of the light, Ida whispered, "Could he be the vessel?"

"No." I sighed. "He is not strong enough. A hard wind would blow him over."

The ghosts of the light-house keepers were restless, as if they sensed the inspector. I saw John standing by the light, or maybe it was just the shadow of him, or a dream.

He seemed to be dancing, like we used to do before he died.

December 9, 1873—

Wind from the south and choppy seas. Given our unanswered letters to the light-house district, we are not terribly concerned about the inspector's threats, and Ida rowed him away at daylight, sending him off without so much as a potato to warm his hands, the scoundrel. When Ida left the island, even just for that moment, the rocks seem to tremble beneath my feet. I do not know if it was the spirits or my own wretched heart. I watched her carefully from the rail with her little telescope, making sure she and the boat came back to me safely.

December 10, 1873—

Winter will be on us soon. The tide is so high that water breaches the island. To get out of the light-house, we must walk across boards strung over the rocks with the sea raging beneath us and whipping our skirts until they are soggy and heavy. Ida sewed herself an oilskin coat out of John's old things; I still have mine in good condition. We set out more planks.

December 13, 1873—

Provisions are low. The supplies have not yet come. Down to one egg and a cup of rice a day. Must send Ida to the cape for supplies, but I am loath to bring it up. Cleaned light and cut firewood.

December 15, 1873—

Frigid morning. The hens escaped in the night. Found one drowned on the rocks, so we ate well tonight, although I like eggs better. Up all night with the confounded oil. John came to me in a dream, and I woke to write down his instructions for keeping the light, but they were all gone from my mind. He was trying to tell me something, but what it was, I have no idea.

December 17, 1873—

Icy rain this morn. Woke yesterday with a head cold. Ida insisted on taking the light. She held a cloth in her hands, and I could see a twin reflection of her in the lens as she focused her attention on wiping it with the glycerin. The lens was almost phosphorescent green. When she came to pat my head with water, I grasped at her hand. She wrapped my hand in her own small hands. I fear I whispered rambling things to her in the fever, but she said nothing of it. Does she know how much I dread losing her—to the sea or to the world, which seems so harsh and far away?

"Let us run away," I think I told her. "Leave this cursed place. Go and find somewhere warm to live, just the two of us."

"Where would we go where we could be more ourselves?" She replied sensibly. "Only alone are we safe, only without the watchful eyes of men."

At least, I think this is what she said. I will ask her in the morning. My eyes are so heavy.

December 19, 1873—

I am much better. The air is full of water. A great storm is coming. Wind fast from across the sea. Trees bending on the far islands. No lights visible as the storm comes on. We carried as many sundries as we could up into the tower, the two of us soaked to the bone and icy cold. Cleaned light, trimmed wicks, brought six tins of oil up.

December 20, 1873—

Terrible storm. Water dashing on the rocks and blasting apart the planks we worked so hard on. We cannot look windward without crying. Four vessels sunk—how many men attached to these, we cannot say. We retrieve two men from the rocks, salt-soaked and addled. Waves roll over where our hen house once stood. I cannot see the graves. I cannot see the garden. All is darkness and water. The lantern rocked as the waves rose to the feet of the keeper's house but did not enter it. All is dark but Ida helps me tend the men with coffee and warmth by the fire. They are uneasy with us and with the ghosts, who I can feel crowding in on us. Our little castle on the water is invaded by the scent of sweat and tobacco and sailors' voices.

Lightning struck the light-house but did no damage. It sounded like a million firearms going off. Shadow the dog hid under the cot.

December 21, 1873—

Bone Light stands. We stand with it, arm to arm, ghost to ghost.

December 22, 1873—

Water receded. I finally admitted we absolutely had to send Ida to get our provisions. For now, we have two men to return to the mainland and very little food left. Ida bundled the men into the boat and rowed away from Bone Light. When she was past the point, she looked back, or at least I thought she did. Before she left, I tucked a list of supplies for the spell for safety into her coat pocket. "Find what you can," I whispered. Most of the items will be easily obtained at the general store on the mainland, but a few may require her to visit the nearby woods around the town of Port Riche. I watched until I could see her boat no longer and tried to tell myself I could not feel the rocks shivering beneath my shoes. Shadow sniffed my hand and then went to lie beside the cot on Ida's side.

December 25, 1873—

I have nearly set the keeper's house to rights from the flood waters. Thankfully, the furniture is of the solid variety of metal and wood and survived with some airing out. What is there to do but maintain this place? I have nothing to decorate with, but Christmas was never the holiday we celebrated when I was a child. Mother used to light the house from top to bottom with candles and a yule log. I am too afraid of fire here for that. I made a little cake with the last of the flour, egg, and dried fruit. Shadow and I ate it, sitting at the top of the tower stairs. I fear those stairs when I am alone. I look down on them and wonder how John came to fall.

December 29, 1873—

Water unsteady and waves high. Ida gone one week. The bodies from the wrecks were never recovered, or at least none have washed up on the shore of our island. I feel fine today without Ida. I can sense the ghosts near me, but I do not feel they mean me any harm, at least not today. Perhaps they are tired from the storm. Cleaned light, set about coating metal to prevent rust.

December 31, 1873—

New Year's Eve. What a wretched, wretched day. Hauled in a small wooden box with the body of an infant nestled inside it. It wore a little bonnet but no blanket. Its blue face was fearful to look upon, the wee thing. Its hands were frozen in time, reaching out for a mother who abandoned it to the sea. I set the box on the table, and

Shadow whined. I cannot row the poor thing to the mainland to alert the authorities with no one to watch the light, not at this time of year. I will dig a grave in the morning. Cleaned light and trimmed wicks.

January 1, 1874—

The New Year dawned cold and dark. Wind howled all around me. The weather has been so wild these last few weeks. The ghosts held the light while I drifted in and out of restless sleep. I saw the ghost of John standing by the light, holding court with the keepers of the past as he once did. His skull was indented where the lamp did him in. I do not think he means me harm, nor do the others who have come to rest on this cursed spit of land. We are all lost souls here. His ghost walked to the table and looked down on the poor child in the box. I tried telling him I never wanted a child, but I would have done it, for you, I would have brought life into this world—but I could not tell if he heard me. My voice went hoarse before I could reach him.

I am lost without Ida. I do not let myself think of her as I trim the wicks, wipe clear the reflector.

January 2, 1874—

The infant body is finally buried. The ground was thick with ice, but I put all of myself into it and managed to break through. All the blisters on my palms burst. Even Shadow helped a little with his claws, but I pushed him away when his paws began to bleed.

I feel certain the babe will not come back, and this gives me some hope. I keep thinking how we will leave no children to treasure our memories. Perhaps my only legacy is the light.

January 5, 1874—

Windy and rough seas. I am sorry to report that some oil was spilled and a fire caught. I put it out with my skirts before it got to the rest of the oil, which is so low I doubt it would have done much damage. My hands badly burned.

I hope Ida brings back cloth for a new skirt as I burned mine to a crisp.

January 10, 1874—

I cannot leave the lantern room all day, for it is foggy, and the light is spiritous. It seems the light is part of myself, a steady beam inside of me, reflecting my soul outward into the night. Before coming here, I was a quiet and steady woman. Now I am riotous on the inside, longing for Ida with a strength that surprises even myself. I dream of the light failing so I have taken to staying up all night until the sweet relief of dawn.

Above all else, we cannot lose the light. I shudder to think what the ghosts would do then.

January 12, 1873—

Three weeks gone by. The sea's voice never quiets. Ghosts walk beside me. Am I becoming one of them? Sometimes I wake and wonder if I am still alive. John lay down beside me, and the cot was so cold, I could feel his hands on my skin. I will love him until the day I die, but I contain so much inside of me, don't I? Leave, I whispered into the pillow. Go on to heaven. But he will not go. Is he angry that I buried the child and gave it to God? Or does he know how I am slowly learning to live without him, day by day?

There is an invisible force between us, and John cannot break that boundary, can he?

I must hold out for Ida. If Bone Light goes down tonight, I go with it.

January 14, 1874—

Ida Boyle writing

I, Ida, write this as Mary sleeps. I found her in the lantern room, her face stricken. She would not speak. I bundled her onto the cot. The light is out, she kept saying, the light is out. And indeed, it was.

The supplies were difficult to obtain on the mainland. I had to visit the office of the Harbormaster and complain. Well, I pretended to be a poorly light-house keeper's wife. When the Harbormaster checked the records, he forgot who Mary was and assumed I was her. I did not bother to correct the man, just insisted on extra supplies. He agreed when he learned "our John" had died, taking sympathy on me finally.

Besides the supplies for the light-house, I went to a little shop off the main street in search of the items for the spell. Mary's scrawling handwriting gave me several suggestions for alternatives, and I was able to obtain most of the needed items, frog's spawn and crystal and crushed limestone, tucked into glass jars.

As I came back from Barnstable, I stopped at Half Moon Point, where I could see the light of Bone Light and thought, I am almost home. The keeper there is a military man and has five rough children, a bewildering brood. His wife invited me to stay the night, and we had tea. He told me of strange happenings at Bone Light—wavering lights on the shore and the dancing of Bone Light as if it were taken by a spirit. I told him he was surely imagining things, but I was terribly worried for Mary.

We looked out at Bone Light. It shone steady, a comforting thing. But as the old mariner and I watched, I imagined Mary tending the light, moving quick as a shot as she always does, and just as I thought this, Bone Light went out. It was out all the rest of the night. The keeper wanted to go in the dark to investigate because the seas were so calm, but I convinced him to let me go in the morning. He helped me load the boat and insisted on coming with me. "This is what comes of letting a woman tend the light," he kept saying. "I was against it from the start." Upon entering the bay, we found three vessels capsized on the reef. I left him, and he stayed to search for bodies.

I rowed like my life depended on it until I reached the island, and Shadow came leaping down the rocks in much distress. He was barking and jumping all around, and his paws were bloody. I tied off the boat and, hitching up my skirts, ran to the light-house. That is when I found Mary.

I cannot tell how terrible it was to see her struck on the floor beside the lamp, which had broken a few panes of glass, an arm over her face. I thought she was dead. It seemed to me that I could hear the voices of the ghosts all around us. I took her in my arms and held her very close. Her eyelids fluttered open, but she could not see me. I looked for the ghosts around us as if for help, but none were near me, and yet they all were near me. And then I realized it. The ghosts are inside of Mary, every one of them. Every soul that ever passed through this cursed place has landed in the skin of my Mary and will not come out.

I shook her hard. "Mary, Mary," I cried. Her eyes would not open. Her breathing was shallow and frail. My strong Mary, buried somewhere in her skin.

It is like the story my mother told me of the woman who went mad. I must set the spell to rights.

We have found our vessel. But will it survive the spell?

January 17, 1874—
Ida Boyle writing

Cleaned light and wiped lens. Mary is awake but still will not speak or cannot. I fear I have lost her forever. She is like a ghost that does not see me. She followed me today with Shadow as I tended to the garden and hens, which were terribly hungry and underfed, not to mention pecking about the garden because their house was destroyed in the storm. I noticed a new grave had been dug since I was last home, and I asked Mary about it, but she only shook her head silently. When I put a box in her hand to carry up from the boat, she carried it but said nothing. She listened when I spoke to her, but she would not say anything. I have three shadows now.

January 23, 1874—

Ida Boyle writing

There is a new ghost among the flock. A baby. I can hear it crying in the night. It follows Mary from place to place and sleeps beside her. I think it is keeping her safe. From what? The ghosts in her skin? Perhaps the baby is like a barrier to them creeping into her soul.

It is the only ghost I have seen since I returned. But I can hear them. They are restless in Mary's eyes. Deep in the depths of her dark brown irises, I sense the presence of men who never grew old, children who did not abide by their parent's rules, the restless souls of the people who lived on this rock far before our country destroyed any hope they had of a future. It is too much.

I set about preparing the spell at once. There must be a circle of stones. Strangely, the storm washed away many of the bones. Bone Light is still partially made of bones, but many of them got swept away or came away from the tower. At the last minute, I amended the spell to include bones in the circle. I spent many hours putting the stone and bone circle right. It must work, this must be right.

Mary has been talking in her sleep. First, her voice goes heavy and deep, and she sounds like John when he was a young man. "Mary, tend the light," she says to herself in his voice. Then, she speaks in the language of the indigenous people, beautiful words that I wish I knew how to respond to, to tell them we are sorry even though we were not the ones who hurt them.

Lastly, she cries like a baby. I do not like this sound.

January 24, 1874——

Ida Boyle writing

I awoke in the darkness with a pounding headache and the urgent feeling that something was wrong. My hands were full of the gray grass that grows here on this island. I realized someone struck me while I was in the garden, searching for stones for the spell circle.

I think it was Mary.

I heard her laughing far in the distance, like she used to laugh, except all twisted like a damaged phonograph, warbling and thin.

I must rest before the spell can be carried out. I am too weak.

January 25, 1874—

Ida Boyle writing

It is done. Whether it worked, I cannot say.

I went in search of Mary but could not find her. I searched and searched the island, walking down to the wet planks by the dock and looking in the boats, both the dinghy and the little sailboat, but they were empty and knocking against each other. I circled the tower, thinking, what if she is following me? But I did not come upon her. Part of me was eaten up with terror that she had slipped and fallen into the sea, and yet the deep gyre in my heart knew she was still with me, somewhere in hiding on the island. Perhaps the Mary part of her that is still there was ashamed at having hurt me.

I locked myself in the lantern room. I looked down on the circle of stones, and as if in a dream, I convinced myself the circle was moving, slowly rippling like a circle of women at a dance, march in file, forward and back a double, sashaying with no men to hold their arms.

I consider myself to be a prudent woman. I do not scare easily. The last time I was so afeared was the day that man took me as a child into the woods. I can still remember how light my body felt as he swung me over his shoulder like a sack of potatoes, the gruff scent of tobacco and shine on his breath, how he said nothing, nothing at all. And then, I could sense Mary in the woods, seeking me. I feel that same sensation now. Like a silent moaning on the breeze, or the sensation I get when the light is on sometimes, and energy seems to arc out of the lens, sending the hairs on my arms straight up.

In some ways, my mother and Mary's mother were mere hedgewitches. Their magick was good for household domesticities. A bumped knee here, a tea for bringing down fever there. Yet I always felt that my mother knew more than she let on. Her mother was from the old country, and after she died, my mother kept a little altar in the room that was meant to be her powder room. It was locked in a wooden dresser, and only she carried the key on a beautiful gold strand at her hip. Sometimes she took me on her lap when I was very little, and she would whisper the words to the spell for safety. It was a lullaby:

My body is too small for safety
Give me a spell for everyone
Whether I live to be eighty
Or die under the midnight sun

My heart is too small for safety
Give me a spell for the whole sky
The daisies and babies and ladies
Goddess, as far as the bird flies

My love is too big for jeopardy
Give me a spell as big as the sea
Put away what darkness lays by
Keep my love under a cool shade tree

My spirit is too wild for refuge
Give me a spell to save the world
Believe power can be this huge
A place so safe my soul unfurls

The spell for safety is a women's fantasy. It's something you whisper to children at night while they sleep. I have found myself many a night since I came here, standing over Mary while she sleeps, whispering the words idly with no intention of them working. For it's foolish women like me who want to believe the world can be a better place.

I kept the light going and decided that upon dawn's first light, I would go to the circle and perform the spell, whether or not Mary decided to make an appearance. I would draw her to me again, like that night in the woods when the man took me.

When dawn's rays crawled their way over the world, the sea was calm. I stood and doused the light. Cautiously, I opened the door to the stairs, and the light-house tower was silent. I locked Shadow in the room behind me. He began to howl, of course, but I daren't let him down while the spell was going on, for he might be hurt. "I'll be back soon, boy," I whispered through the crack in the door, but I didn't believe myself. My voice sounded ghostlike to me, thin and wavery.

I ducked into the keeper's house and put on my apron, filling my pockets with the necessary ingredients for the

132

spell. There was no sign of Mary in the garden. I went to the stones and saw they had all been thrown at angles in the night, as if a giant had come along and smacked the circle open. Kneeling in the cold dirt, I gathered them back in my apron and deposited them again in a circle. Then, I went to the center and made a small fire. There I burned the ingredients for the spell and, taking up a little knife, cut the center of my palms and the place on my head where the third eye resides.

Although it was daytime, the day was dark and grim. The sea was very quiet. I closed my eyes and called out to Mary with the inner light inside of me. I felt nothing for many minutes. Then a strange feeling like I was being watched, and shortly after that, a tug at my belly like an arrow shot. I turned and saw Mary walking up the rocks. She was a dark figure against the gray mist, her dress soaked, her hair plastered to her head, her smile a bright cut in her face. She paused outside the stones and tilted her head eerily to one side as if asking for permission to come in. I nodded, breathing in the harsh smoke, my throat constricting.

Once she was in, she smiled, paused, and launched herself at me.

She had an object in her hand, I did not know what at first—until I saw it was a bone. A jawbone. She struck out at me with it, and I spun, whirling away, but then she grabbed my skirt and yanked me back, screaming, "Get over here, thee foolish woman!" in the voice of a man. I spun again, my skirt ripping in her hands. I heard the baby cry again and felt a moment of lightness, and I grappled with Mary. I needed to maintain contact for the spell to work. She fought me, hard, her eyes shifting as the souls inside of her came to the surface and battled to control her.

"I know you're in there, Mary!" I hissed, and she hit me aside the head.

I went sprawling across the ground but caught myself before I could break the circle.

"Little hedgewhore!" Mary straddled me and brought the jawbone high above her.

The little child became real, its soul materializing between us. Hovering in the air, it brought up its little arm, and Mary wheeled away, screaming in her own voice. She screamed and screamed.

"Help me," I whispered to the child, which was silly because how could a baby help me?

But at the sound of my voice, Mary's body jerked. A light flashed in her eyes and then went dark.

Her John leaped from her body and materialized beside me. "I have you, Ida," I heard him call into the wind, which had picked up and was whipping my tattered skirts in a frenzy. I don't think the man ever said my name once in his whole life. I reached out my two hands, one to the baby, one to John. His hand was warm in mine. He looked me in the eyes, and I saw there the truth—that he knew what had passed between Mary and myself. Perhaps he'd always known who we are, what we are. He smiled and nodded, a kind of half-shrug, as if to say, *I'm sorry I could not get to you sooner.* Or else, *Well, what is a man to do?*

"Help me," I called out one more time. Now my voice was stronger, more sure.

Another spirit jumped free of Mary's body, the spirit of a girl with braids in her hair and a round belly. Barely old enough to bear a child, she held a great hoop in her hands that seemed to be made of light. She placed it over me and it settled around my hips, and she rubbed one hand across her belly.

Together, the ghosts and I stepped toward Mary. She flattened herself against the stone circle, but she could not get out. Her back bowed against an invisible dome; her breathing was ragged. I reached forward, the two ghostly hands on the back of mine. It felt as though I was reaching into molasses, but I managed to get a grip on Mary's hands. I yanked them up, intertwining my fingers in hers. The hoop of light vibrated around my hips, the young pregnant mother holding onto it.

"Now you listen to me, Mary mine, I'm not going to let you go," I said fiercely. "So long as I have breath in my lungs and a beat in my heart, I'm not going to let you go."

Mary's back arched, and her eyes rolled back in their sockets, grim white. But she did not let go.

"Spirits of Bone Light," I called. "You have too long haunted this place. There is nothing left to fight for here. This place is not meant to be a dark place. It's meant to live!" Then I began to say the words of the spell for safety. As each word dropped from my mouth, I could feel something let go of Mary. In my mind's eye, I saw the whole long, wretched history of the place and the way it once was before the great massacre, before humans ever touched this rock. I saw the families who had lived here over the years, the spirits whose deaths slowly added to the darkness of the place. So many spirits on one spit of land.

Is it any wonder it became so? John stood by my side holding the little babe as, one by one, the spirits dropped their hold of Mary and left, spinning out over the water like the beam of the light. I just stood there, sweat dripping down my neck, my hands clenched in Mary's, refusing to let go.

When the spell was complete, a great light settled over us. It rippled out over the water. I closed my eyes. Mary fell into my arms.

The baby looked over John's arm, into Mary's face, like a curious cat. Then it patted her cheek and was gone. I suppose I'll never know how its soul came to be at Bone Light.

The young pregnant woman touched the hoop of light at my waist and it dissipated. She ran a hand over her belly again, wistfully, then gave me a small smile before departing, one that I like to think said, *You did not save us, but I thank you anyway.*

I dragged Mary to the little bed in the dwelling at the base of the light-house. She was dead asleep but breathing normally. I took off her wet things and tucked her into the bed, wrapping her up in her mother's quilt.

Somehow, the spell had taken the entire day. I have not much memory of the time.

I have been unable to sleep since the spell. I have been tending the light, looking out over the sea, expecting the darkness to return. But the night is clear. The oil burns clean.

Mary's John sits by the light, his hands restless with nothing to do, looking at me like he will always be there between us. I must do something. I went to the light while Mary slept, and I tried to think of how to cast him away. Then I realized that was not what I was after. Finally, I spoke to him. It seemed the most sensible thing to do. I told him how I loved Mary, and I'd take care of her, and how he didn't have to worry.

He put his hands in his pockets and looked up at something I couldn't see. He seemed to hear a voice inaudible to my human senses. He walked to the light and looked back, his face a little sheepish. He nodded to me once. Then he was gone.

I wouldn't have believed it of him to go just like that, but then again, he always was a sensible soul.

January 26, 1874—
Ida Boyle writing

The morning came clear and bright. Mary is slowly thawing. I was trimming the wicks as the pink rays of dawn touched the sea, and she stood by the rail, looking out over the water. I have been nervous about losing her again, so I tied a rope from her waist to mine.

She turned and seemed to see me then. "Ida, is that you?" she said.

"Yes, it's your Ida," I said.

"My Ida," she repeated in a soft voice.

She was quiet the rest of the day, but her eyes were hers. No unmoored souls thrashed in them, nothing trapped in her skin.

January 27, 1874—
Ida Boyle writing

We have all the stores unloaded now. The dwelling is dry, and I have completed most of the repairs after the storm. We will need a new hen house, and the stairs of the light-house tower could use repainting. I brought most of what we need, and I received my letter of commission appointing me to assistant keeper. I suppose the inspector never got his wish of replacing us with a man.

I have decided we will replace the holes in the tower with stones. Let the sea claim its own.

No more words from Mary yet.

I have not seen John again.

February 6, 1874—
Ida Boyle writing

Glorious sunny day. This morning Mary was up filling the lamp. When I sat up on the cot, feeling the loss of her warmth, she smiled at me. "Good morning, Ida," she said. She seems to have no memory of her ordeal. We ate beans and rice while Shadow played, chasing one of the hens.

"We will write to my brother and ask him to come stay so that we may take a trip away," Mary said to me as she watched Shadow play. "We are allowed a holiday of twenty-four hours, after all. I think we should go to town and go to the opera house there."

I was so happy to hear her voice again that I agreed on the spot.

When I went to check on the light, I found it glowing warm and radiant. The walls were no longer whispering. Bone Light is quiet tonight.

ABOUT THE AUTHORS

D. MATTHEW URBAN hails from Texas and lives in Queens, NY, where he reads weird books, watches weird movies, and writes weird fiction. His stories can be found in *No Trouble at All* (Cursed Morsels Press), *The First Five Minutes of the Apocalypse* (Hungry Shadow Press), and *Monster Lairs* (Dark Matter INK), among other venues. Find him on Twitter @breathinghead or on the web at dmatthewurban.com.

HOLLY LYN WALRATH is a writer, editor, and publisher. Her poetry and short fiction has appeared in Strange Horizons, Fireside Fiction, Analog, and Flash Fiction Online. She is the author of several books of poetry including Glimmerglass Girl (2018), Numinose Lapidi (2020), and The Smallest of Bones (2021). She holds a B.A. in English from The University of Texas and a Master's in Creative Writing from the University of Denver.

ABOUT THE ARTISTS

Viviana is a Portuguese artist most known as **ECHO ECHO**. Her creative influence is born in observing nature to the smallest details and recreating that feeling in her illustrations. She likes to create new worlds, bringing some sort of reality to these fantasy worlds while filling them with psychedelic manifestations of her imagination. Find more of her work on Instagram @echoechoillustrations.

EVANGELINE GALLAGHER is an award-winning illustrator from Baltimore, Maryland. They received their BFA in Illustration from the Maryland Institute College of Art in 2018. When they aren't drawing they're probably hanging out with their dog, Charlie, or losing at a board game. They possess the speed and enthusiasm of 10,000 illustrators.

ACKNOWLEDGMENTS

D. MATTHEW URBAN – Thanks to this story's first readers, my parents and sisters, whose comments on a very messy first draft went above and beyond the call of familial duty. Thanks to Celina, the love of my life, for laughing at the funny parts. Thanks to my critique partners at Brooklyn Speculative Fiction Writers, who didn't read this particular piece (too long for a short story—the curse of the novelette!) but whose feedback and encouragement have benefited my writing tremendously, despite my interloping from another borough. Thanks to Alex Ebenstein for expert editing that helped whip this strange story into shape. Thanks, finally, to Mrs. Giles, my high school Latin teacher, who taught me many years ago that sometimes all it takes to reanimate a dead language is a little imagination.

CONTENT WARNINGS

These stories are works of horror fiction which contain dark content that may be triggering to some individuals. In addition to instances and implications of violence and death throughout, there are instances of child death and infertility in "Bone Light." Please read with caution.

TENEBROUS PRESS

aims to drag the malleable Horror genre into newer, Weirder territory with stories that are incisive, provocative, intelligent and terrifying; delivered by voices diverse and unsung.

FIND OUT MORE:
www.tenebrouspress.com
Social Media @TenebrousPress

NEW WEIRD HORROR

TENEBROUS

10p

PRESS

Printed in the USA
CPSIA information can be obtained
at www.ICGtesting.com
JSHW080727211023
50385JS00004B/24